E.

Earthquake!

LEFT BEHIND
>THE KIDS<

Jerry B. Jenkins

Tim LaHaye

WITH CHRIS FABRY

TYNDALE HOUSE PUBLISHERS, INC.
WHEATON, ILLINOIS

YA
JEN

Visit Tyndale's exciting Web site at www.tyndale.com

Discover the latest Left Behind news at www.leftbehind.com

Left Behind is a registered trademark of Tyndale House Publishers, Inc.

Published in association with the literary agency of Alive Communications, Inc., 7680 Goddard Street, Suite 200, Colorado Springs, CO 80920.

Edited by Curtis H. C. Lundgren

ISBN 0-8423-4332-6

Printed in the United States of America

08 07 06 05 04 03 02 01
11 10 9   8   7   6   5   4   3

To Kaitlyn Nicole

TABLE OF CONTENTS

What's Gone On Before ix

1. The Bridge 9:22 A.M. 1

2. The Wrath of the Lamb 9:37 A.M. . . 15

3. Fire from Heaven 9:45 A.M. 27

4. The Aftermath 9:51 A.M.. 41

5. Lionel's Problem 12:36 P.M.. 55

6. Shelly's Story 1:22 P.M. 69

7. Helping Pete 2:13 P.M. 83

8. Ryan's Bad News 4:08 P.M. 97

9. Chaya's Last Chance 5:52 P.M.. . . 111

10. Decision Time 9:22 P.M. 125

    Epilogue 137

    About the Authors

What's Gone On Before

JUDD Thompson Jr. and the other kids in the Young Tribulation Force are involved in the adventure of a lifetime. The global vanishings have left them alone.

After a dangerous trip to Israel, Judd goes into hiding from the Global Community and discovers hidden documents. Before he can use the documents to rescue his friends, Judd is taken to GC headquarters. Judd and the pilot, Taylor Graham, are on their way to a reeducation facility when they notice dead animals on the road.

Lionel Washington is told he has family in the South. Instead, he is taken to a Global Community camp for young people. While others seem to be brainwashed, Lionel goes along, hoping he can escape and rejoin his friends. Lionel sees the ground of the compound filled with snakes. He feels the rumble and realizes there is no place to hide.

Vicki Byrne is desperate to deliver copies of

the *Underground* that predicts a global earthquake. She is caught by the principal, Mrs. Jenness, who drives Vicki to the authorities.

Vicki's friend, Chaya Stein, looks among her mother's belongings for a keepsake. Her father returns home as bits of plaster fall from the ceiling.

Ryan Daley has promised he won't go outside, but his dog Phoenix is going crazy. He lets the dog out at the moment of the earth's most violent earthquake.

The Young Trib Force is scattered, scared, and in great danger.

ONE

The Bridge

9:22 A.M.

VICKI sat in horror as the bridge wobbled and buckled. Mrs. Jenness slammed on the brakes and covered her eyes.

"Make it stop," Mrs. Jenness whimpered.

A few minutes earlier, Mrs. Jenness had been gloating over catching Vicki with a new edition of the *Underground*. Vicki knew she was headed back to the detention center, or possibly worse. Now both were hanging on for their lives.

Vicki checked to be sure the windows were up, in case the bridge collapsed and they fell into the water.

"Back up!" Vicki shouted.

"Make it stop!" Mrs. Jenness said.

Vicki heard the thundering of the great earthquake. It roared like a thousand cannons. The normally calm river rushed by with whitecaps as the bridge rocked.

Vicki decided to jump out and run, but

1

before she could get the door unlocked, the bridge tipped violently and the car rolled on its top. The windshield shattered. Shards of glass flew everywhere.

They came to rest on the railing, the front of the car over the edge. Several cars toppled into the water. One man had gotten out of his vehicle and raced for safety. A few steps later and he was in the air, flying headlong into the choppy water.

How could the bridge last this long? If they fell with the bridge, the twisted metal and concrete would drag them down. The bridge tipped, then slammed the car against the railing again. Metal scraped against concrete. The back tires rose off the pavement. Vicki and Mrs. Jenness screamed as they plunged over the edge.

The car landed back end first but didn't sink. Water poured in through the broken windows, then the car settled. The current took them underneath the bridge, chunks of asphalt and steel plopping in the water around them.

The water reached Vicki's feet and took her breath away. Mrs. Jenness looked terrified, and she shook uncontrollably. Vicki couldn't help feeling sorry for her.

"We're gonna get out of this," Vicki said.

"I can't swim!" Mrs. Jenness screamed.

The earthquake rolled on as the car spun in the river. Water continued to rise through the floor. As the car sank, Vicki unbuckled herself and Mrs. Jenness.

"Crawl on top," Vicki shouted. "I'll help you make it to shore."

Mrs. Jenness stared past Vicki and pointed. A downed tree stuck out over the water. The car rushed toward it.

"Get down!" Vicki yelled.

The treetop rammed through the opening of the back window and stopped within inches of Mrs. Jenness's head. The car hung by the tree, a foot above the surface of the water.

"We have to get out," Vicki said. "If the tree breaks, we're dead. And if the water level rises, the tree will hold us under."

"Stay here," Mrs. Jenness said. "Wait for help."

Vicki noticed a red gash on the woman's forehead. She must have hit the steering wheel hard. Part of Vicki wanted to leave her. Mrs. Jenness had been no end of trouble for the Young Trib Force. But something inside wouldn't let her.

"We go together," Vicki said. "I'll get out and pull you through the other side."

Vicki struggled through the window. The car top was crushed. She cut her hand on a piece of glass that clung to the windshield, but she didn't let go. The river rose, and the rushing water and trembling earth were deafening.

When she got to Mrs. Jenness, Vicki looked back in horror as the bridge collapsed. Huge concrete pylons snapped like twigs. Cars were trapped in the twisting metal. Vicki braced herself as a huge wave swept over them and nearly knocked her off. When the wave passed, Vicki coughed and saw the water pouring in the windows.

"Give me your hand!" Vicki shouted above the noise.

Then it happened. Darkness. The sun went black. Vicki heard the roar of the earth and water, but she saw nothing. She felt helpless.

Vicki hung on to the roof as another violent rumble nearly shook the tree loose. A cracking, an explosion, and another deafening shake sent the water swirling around them. Vicki reached into the car and realized the water level was going down.

"You still there?" Vicki screamed.

"I think so," came the weak reply.

"Turn on your lights!" Vicki yelled.

The beams cut through the darkness. Vicki blinked and wiped her eyes. She couldn't believe it. The earth had opened from one side of the river to the other into a bottomless chasm. Water cascaded into the hole but didn't fill it. It looked like the hole just kept going to the center of the earth. The riverbed was changing, and water from both sides of the crevice rushed in. If they fell into the hole, they would never be found. If they fell into the water on either side of the chasm, the current would drag them into it as well.

The car shifted, and Vicki nearly lost her balance. She turned as a flash lit the sky and revealed a scene Vicki would never forget. The tree roots barely clung to a wall of shifting earth. Below her was black nothingness.

"Help me," Vicki muttered. "Please, God . . ."

Judd Thompson had noticed the dead animals along the road to the reeducation facility. The GC pilot he had come to trust, Taylor Graham, sat beside him in the GC transport van. Both were handcuffed. Taylor had been beaten during his time in custody, and Judd could tell he was weak. The two were on their way to a maximum 5 facility when the great earthquake began.

Judd noticed flagpoles and weather vanes rocking as they passed through the farmlands of central Illinois. Squirrels, rabbits, dogs, cats, and deer darted back and forth. People were used to seeing raccoons and opossums dead on the road, but now it was every kind of animal. Lifeless bodies were strewn about the road.

The driver swerved to miss a Great Dane, and the road in front of the van buckled and heaved upward.

"Hang on!" Taylor screamed.

The van went airborne. Judd held on to the seat in front of him as they crashed to the pavement. He found himself suspended by his seat belt as the van skidded to a stop. But the earth seemed to pick up momentum.

Taylor Graham unbuckled himself and kicked open the emergency exit. Judd followed. He smelled gasoline.

"Good thing they didn't put us in leg irons," Taylor said.

"What about them?" Judd said, pointing to the driver and the other guard. Both men were in the front of the van. Neither moved.

"You're right," Taylor said. "We need the keys to these handcuffs."

Before Taylor could get to them, an explosion ripped through the van and set the vehicle ablaze. Judd and Taylor were thrown into a ditch.

"We'll never get them now," Taylor said. "Come on. We'll find a place that's safe."

As they ran toward a cornfield, Judd tried to balance himself. It felt like he was walking on the deck of a ship in a hurricane.

The sound was incredible. When he had been mad at his parents he would go into his room and turn his headphones up full blast. This was louder, and there was no turning down the volume.

Judd glanced back as a huge crater opened. The burning van and a section of road were swallowed whole. Black smoke rose from the wreckage. Nearby a farmhouse vanished. Horses ran in circles in their corral.

"When's this thing gonna stop?" Taylor shouted.

Judd heard crumpling metal and saw power lines. The towers fell, the deadly lines crashing with them.

"Look out!" Judd yelled.

When the sun went black, Judd couldn't see his hands in front of his face. He heard crackling nearby.

"Don't move," Taylor said.

Judd's heart beat furiously. One wrong step and they could be killed instantly.

A flash lit the sky, and Judd saw the power lines only a few feet away.

"To your left," Taylor said, and the two struggled to their feet.

Lionel Washington was in the exercise yard near the main compound building when the great earthquake began. He had been told he had family who wanted to care for him. That was a lie. What he found in this secluded Alabama town was a Global Community training camp. Lionel and the others were being groomed as monitors. The camp leaders called them the "eyes and ears of Nicolae Carpathia."

Lionel hated the idea of helping the Global Community, but pretending to go along with them was his only chance. More than anything he wanted to get back to his friends in Mount Prospect. If that meant memorizing a few GC chants and faking obedience, he'd do it.

Someone in camp noticed a horde of snakes slithering across the compound. Moments later, Lionel felt the ground rumble. He turned to run inside a building, then stopped. A friend ran past him.

"Don't go in there, Conrad!" Lionel yelled.

Conrad kept going. Lionel followed, screaming for the boy to stop. Lionel caught him on the stairwell, grabbed his arm, and turned for the front door.

"What're you doing?" Conrad said.

"Earthquake!" Lionel said. "We have to get out!"

Conrad ran. Lionel followed. The hardwood floor vibrated. He was almost outside when the beams on the porch gave way. Lionel shoved Conrad to safety as the porch crashed down on him.

After almost being caught by the Global Community, Ryan Daley promised Vicki he would stay inside. But when Phoenix bounded into his basement hideout, barking and running in circles, Ryan figured the dog needed to go out. He opened the back door and watched Phoenix scamper around the yard. The dog sniffed at the air and took off again.

At first, Ryan thought he heard a train. But there were no tracks near Vicki's house. He ran into the kitchen as cabinets opened, spilling dishes and glasses.

What do I do? Ryan wondered. *Go to the basement? Upstairs? Outside?*

He dove under the kitchen table as a light fell from the ceiling. Through the sliding glass door he saw the ground moving. A neighbor's in-ground pool cracked and collapsed. A huge oak tree in the backyard leaned to one side, then reversed and crashed into the house, the roots tearing up the yard. Phoenix darted back and forth.

"Run, Phoenix!" Ryan shouted.

Then darkness.

Pitch black.

Ryan rolled from under the table and snatched a flashlight from the utility drawer. He switched it on and screamed. The kitchen floor cracked. Pieces of tile snapped and hit him in the face. He tried to roll to the opposite side as the floor heaved upward, then tilted. Ryan grabbed the leg of a chair as he slipped through the opening. The flashlight fell and smacked into something hard. The chair he clung to wedged on each side of the crack. Ryan hung in the air, peering into what had been the basement. Cracked concrete and rocks filled the room.

Above him darkness. Below him the tiny beam of the flashlight.

Another shift and the chair snapped. Ryan fell into the churning debris.

Chaya Stein had gone to her father's house with mixed emotions. Her mother had died in the same blast that had killed Bruce

Barnes. Chaya wanted a keepsake from her mother. Chaya's father didn't want to see her and asked that she be gone by 9:00 A.M.

At 9:18 Chaya heard someone in the front room. Mr. Stein spoke sharply. Chaya knew her father was still angry that she believed in Jesus as the Messiah.

A chunk of plaster hit Chaya. A rumble rolled beneath her.

Mr. Stein stood in the doorway, ready to leave.

Chaya screamed, "It's coming!"

She grabbed the railing with both hands and held on. A chandelier in the front room fell, just missing Mr. Stein. The railing cracked and sent Chaya over the edge to the floor.

The ceiling gave way as Mr. Stein rushed toward her. A huge beam fell and landed on her legs, crunching the bones. The other end of the beam smashed into the grand piano, splintering it to pieces. Bricks from the fireplace littered the floor.

Through the dust and noise, Chaya's father yelled her name. He staggered into the room, horror on his face.

"I'll get you out!" he said.

Before he could move, the ceiling collapsed, raining boards and plaster. The room was white with dust. Chaya screamed for her father to save himself, but he didn't answer.

A beautiful morning had transformed into darkness. Chaya shivered as she struggled to move. The beam had her legs pinned. Her father lay under rubble only a few feet away. And she heard nothing but the most fierce earthquake in history.

Darrion Stahley was lonely. Her mother had been arrested a full week ago, and Darrion felt powerless to help. Darrion had been brought to Donny and Sandy Moore's house for safety. Early that Monday morning she chatted with Sandy. Donny was heading to the church. Just talking with the Moores made Darrion feel better.

Mrs. Moore had lost a baby in the disappearances. She and Donny said they looked forward to seeing their child in heaven someday.

Darrion left Sandy eating her breakfast and reading the paper. Darrion retreated into the shelter Mr. Moore had built under the house. It wasn't finished, but Darrion was able to relax there.

Darrion was angry at her mother for getting arrested. They could have gone back to their cottage in Wisconsin and no one would have known. Now her mom was in the custody of the Global Community, falsely accused of murdering her husband.

As Darrion thought about ways to help her mother escape, she heard a rumbling. The room began to shake. She screamed for Mrs. Moore, then heard a crash above. The floor of the basement caved in. The limbs of a tree pushed through a hole in the kitchen floor.

Darrion pulled the door of the shelter closed. She knelt with the earth shaking violently around her, and she wept with fear.

TWO

The Wrath
of the Lamb

9:37 A.M.

VICKI held on. It was the only thing she could do. She was on top of Mrs. Jenness's car, her feet touching the tree that held them suspended over the chasm. The car rocked as Vicki moved slightly.

Though she couldn't see in the dark, she knew her only chance of escape was the tree. If she could make her way back along the trunk to its base, there was a chance she could climb up the bank to safety. She gingerly leaned down to the driver's window.

"Mrs. Jenness, you have to climb out," Vicki screamed. "It's the only way."

"I can't," the woman said. "I'll wait until the rescue squad comes."

"There isn't gonna be a rescue squad," Vicki said. "Can't you see? This is the world-wide quake the Bible predicted. This is what I wrote about in the *Underground*."

Mrs. Jenness held the steering wheel. Her knuckles were white. Vicki had to make a decision. If the woman didn't want help, Vicki would have to leave without her.

"Please," Vicki pleaded, "give me your hand."

"Leave me," Mrs. Jenness said.

Vicki scooted back on the roof of the car and grabbed the tree trunk. Water sprayed up from the chasm. The tree was slick.

She was only a few feet along the tree when another fierce tremor sent the ground rolling behind her. The earth swallowed the tree roots, and Vicki held on as she was moved downstream. The car submerged. Vicki was underwater before she could take a good breath of air. She held on to a small limb, surfaced for air, then pulled herself toward the car.

In the inky blackness, she felt her way down. The current was swift, and if she hadn't had the tree and the car to hold on to, she would have been swept to her death. The car lights flickered underwater. Vicki reached inside the driver's side. She found the steering wheel. Then she touched a lifeless hand. Mrs. Jenness. In the reflection of the dashboard light, she saw the tree had struck the principal in the head.

She must have been killed instantly when the car went under, Vicki thought.

For a moment, Vicki froze. She knew it would be easier to give up. But something willed her to fight.

Then Vicki realized the water current and the gaping hole weren't the worst dangers she faced. The water was. Her hands were almost numb, and she could hardly feel her legs. With all the strength she could muster, Vicki struggled to the surface. She grabbed a limb and pulled herself up.

She slowly crawled along the length of the tree until she felt the muddy bank. She climbed the last of the roots to the top of the embankment hollowed out by the earthquake. The sky was changing now, and Vicki saw the submerged car. She looked toward the city, but there were no lights. Screams and cries echoed into the watery canyon. People staggered by in tattered clothes. A man in a suit and tie ran by in muddy shoes. He called out for his wife. Vicki cried for help but no one responded.

Vicki made her way back far enough from the bank to be safe, but another shock sent the ground at her feet crumbling into the water. The tree finally dislodged and fell into the water with a great splash. The current turned the tree around, then flipped the car onto its top. Both plunged into the chasm.

Vicki cried. She cried for Mrs. Jenness. She cried for others who were facing death. And she cried for herself.

Did you bring me through all that's happened to let me die in an earthquake? Vicki prayed.

Nothing. Just the mighty churning water and the rumbling earth that would not stop.

Judd and Taylor felt their way along in the darkness, their handcuffs clacking. Away from the electric lines, they were at least safe from electrocution. But the earth kept moving. Judd never knew when the next step might lead him into a newly opened hole.

"At least we're safe from things falling on us here," Judd said.

"Safe is a relative term," Taylor said. "You say this thing was predicted in the Bible?"

"If you'd have stuck around for the service for Bruce," Judd said, "you would have heard about this. I downloaded Tsion Ben-Judah's take on it."

"What's he say?" Taylor said.

Judd thought about the rabbi in his shelter at the church and wondered if he had survived. If it was a worldwide quake, Buck, Chloe,

Amanda, and Rayford had to be caught in it as well.

"The Bible calls this the wrath of the Lamb," Judd said. "The Lamb is Jesus Christ. The Bible says the sun will be black and the moon will become like blood."

"Sure got the sun right," Taylor said. "Can't see the moon. What else?"

"I can't remember all of it," Judd said. "There's something about the mountains moving and people hiding in caves and asking God to kill them. . . ."

A section of earth gave way near Judd. He sat rigid until he felt it was safe to move. "That was a close one," Judd said.

Taylor didn't respond.

"Taylor?" Judd shouted. "Where are you?"

Something groaned beneath Judd. The wind picked up and blew dust into his eyes. When he could see again, clouds rolled back and a huge crater appeared inches from his feet.

At the bottom of the crater, Taylor Graham lay in a heap. Judd shouted to him, but the pilot didn't move. With the ground shifting, he couldn't risk going after Taylor.

Judd looked around for help. He was near the house that had disappeared. A tire swing hung from a tree a hundred yards away, but between Judd and the tree lay another huge gorge.

Judd looked at the sky and gasped. He suddenly remembered the rest of the passage.

The stars of heaven fell to the earth!

Lionel put up his hands as the porch roof crashed down. He fell backward. Support beams landed near him. If one had hit his head, he knew he would have died instantly. Wood splinters scratched his arms and tore his pants.

"Lionel," Conrad called, "can you hear me?"

"Don't come in here," Lionel yelled. "Get away from the building!"

The second floor caved in behind Lionel, and he could hear the screams of the dying. Lionel dug his way to the front door. He coughed and tried to get air, but there was so much dust he had to put his shirt over his face to breathe. There was no light. No way to see which way to go.

The earth shook with such force that Lionel thought he would be killed any minute. It was a miracle any part of the building still stood.

This was his chance. If he could get out of the house, he could make a break for it. Maybe take Conrad with him and explain the truth about the Global Community and what the Bible said was happening.

Through the shaking, Lionel found the stairwell and sat in the doorway. If there was any hope of safety, it was here.

A beam of light trembled with each rattle of the earth. Then a horn.

"Lionel, can you hear me?" Conrad yelled from a car. "Follow the headlights to find your way out!"

Lionel moved toward the light and found the biggest opening he could. He clawed at boards and rocks. The rumbling and shifting continued. Lionel heard Conrad clearing debris from the other side. As Lionel fell out of the rubble, another shock sent them both back to the ground. The headlights turned skyward as the car sank into the ground. The building collapsed behind Lionel.

A whistling, like air escaping.

"Gas leak!" Conrad said.

An explosion rocked the compound. Lionel and Conrad were thrown from the blast, along with the shattered building. Lionel landed in the dirt. Monstrous black and purple clouds formed in the sky.

Ryan braced himself to hit concrete as he fell into the basement. He imagined landing headfirst and splitting his head open. Instead, he twisted in the air and landed on his back. Something cracked, and he felt a sharp pain. Then nothing.

The earth shifted again, and Ryan was rolled over. He lost his breath as something slammed onto his back. He panicked, struggling for air and to get out from under the heavy load. When he couldn't, he settled and slowly regained his breath. There was pressure on his chest but no pain. He tried to move again.

I'll just wait a minute, he thought. *When the earth moves again, I'll get out.*

But the thing on his back didn't move. The pressure grew worse. It was hard to breathe. Then he heard dripping. The flashlight was a few feet away, but Ryan couldn't reach it. He felt around in the mud and found a splintered piece of wood. By scraping it against the flashlight, he pulled it close.

He shone the light on what was left of the basement wall. A stream of water rolled down the side and collected in a pool. The water pipes had burst. If Ryan didn't get out from under whatever was on his back, he could drown in less than two feet of water. The rumblings sounded different down here. Above ground the noise spread out. In the basement, the sound was like the beating of a drum, and the drum was the earth.

He turned the flashlight and craned his neck. A huge slab pressed into his back. He tried to move his legs. Nothing.

Ryan scratched at the mud and clay beneath. It would take him hours to dig out. The shifting ground might crush him by then. Or the water might be over his head.

He had to try. Ryan used the flashlight and dug with all his might.

Chaya struggled to free herself, but the weight of the beam was too much. Broken glass fell around her as the earthquake rolled on. She could hear the screams of people in the street. She screamed too. Furniture from the second floor toppled down. She tried to cover herself, but with each shudder of the earth, more things fell.

She called out for her father over the noise. Finally, he answered.

"I am here," Mr. Stein said. "Are you safe?"

"I can't move," Chaya said. "I think my legs are broken. And you?"

"I will try to get you out," he said. "Keep talking so I can find you."

Chaya softly sang a song from her childhood. Her mother had sung it to her at bedtime. Tears rolled down her cheeks as she choked out the melody.

"Do you remember that song?" she yelled.

"I do," Mr. Stein said. "I wish your mother was here with us now."

Chaya could hear her father moving in the rubble nearby. "She is in a much better place," Chaya said.

The movement stopped. "What are you saying?" her father said. "You do not wish your mother was here?"

A wall behind Chaya fell outward. Bedroom furniture spilled into the yard.

"I am only saying that I am glad Mother is in heaven now and doesn't have to go through this," Chaya said.

Mr. Stein resumed his search.

"I have not been able to talk with you about this," Chaya said. "You would not speak to me."

Mr. Stein was close. Chaya felt a piece of wood lift from her shoulder.

"Talk to me about what?" Mr. Stein said.

"That day at the hospital," Chaya said. "Before she died she wrote something. She was holding it in her hand. It was a prayer."

"Your mother always wrote things," Mr. Stein said. "Put out your hand. See if you can reach me."

Chaya lifted her arm and strained. She felt her father's fingertips in the darkness.

"A little farther," Mr. Stein said.

"Mother gave her life to God before she died," Chaya said. "She believed in Jesus."

Mr. Stein's hand went limp. Another surge of the earthquake brought a cascade of debris onto them. Chaya lost her father's hand. She screamed. He did not answer.

Darrion prayed for her life. She prayed for Ryan and Judd. She prayed for Vicki. For Chaya. For Taylor Graham and especially for her mother. When the electricity went out, she was in total darkness. The shelter had no windows, but through the ventilation shaft she could hear what was happening outside.

People ran from their homes screaming. The earthquake was so sudden, Darrion couldn't imagine anyone being able to react in time. Then she thought of Sandy and Donny Moore. She crawled on hands and knees to the massive shelter door. It was like trying to walk on a moving teeter-totter. She managed to get the door open a few inches, but something had fallen on the other side.

"Mrs. Moore!!" Darrion screamed.

No answer.

Donny will come for us, Darrion thought. *He'll get us out of here.*

Darrion closed the door and crawled under her bed. The quake was rearranging what little furniture there was in the shelter.

Please, God, Darrion prayed, *help me get out of here alive.*

THREE

Fire from Heaven

9:45 A.M.

VICKI trembled. The sky was changing, and for the first time she saw the wreckage clearly. Beautiful houses toppled into the river. People ran screaming into the street. Some fell into huge cracks in the earth. Others seemed to want to die. The quake roared on and on. Like a hungry beast, it devoured everything in its path.

Great mounds of asphalt shot upward. What Vicki couldn't climb over, she went around. It was slow, but she figured her chances of survival were better if she kept moving.

But where was she going? An hour ago she sat in Mrs. Jenness's office and watched her read the *Underground*. Now the woman was dead, and Vicki was fighting for her life. She wanted to find the others. Just one friend.

Traffic signs, streetlights, and telephone poles were gone. Vicki saw a row of apartment buildings. Only one stood above ground. The others had collapsed or had been swallowed whole by the earth.

Vicki walked over two yellow humps barely sticking out of the ground, then realized it was all that was left of a fast-food restaurant. Across the street, cars were piled on top of each other at a car dealership. A computer store stood at a jagged angle, then slowly the walls caved in.

A bell rang behind her, and Vicki turned to see the steeple of a church crash to the ground. She wondered about her own church and who might be there. Loretta? The rabbi? Had anyone else survived? What about her school?

Then Vicki remembered Ryan. She had insisted he stay inside. Could he still be alive? A wave of guilt stopped Vicki and she knelt. *I have to get back there and find him,* she thought.

When the car had plunged into the water, Vicki could only think about getting out alive. Now she thought about the others. Where was Lionel? Was Chaya driving home from her father's house when the earthquake hit? And Judd. Where was Judd in all of this?

Though the streets had no signs, she knew she was a few miles from home. But it might as well have been a few hundred miles. Walking through the shifting rubble was next to impossible.

No emotions, Vicki thought. *I have to stay alive. Just get back to the house and find Ryan.*

The sky peeled back, and monstrous black and purple clouds hovered over the town. It looked like a horror movie.

Then it began.

Huge flaming rocks streaked to earth. The sky was falling, and it was on fire. Vicki covered her eyes. It had gone from day to night and now back to day with the glowing balls of fire.

The earth was still rolling under her feet. Vicki had to stay upright and avoid the hurtling meteors. They seemed to smash everything the earthquake hadn't swallowed.

The heat from the meteors was intense. The smell was overwhelming. When a meteor slammed into the ground, it exploded and sent molten rock flying. Vicki looked at the horizon and saw an incredible sight. Thousands of red streaks descended from the darkness above, pounding the ground with yellow bursts of light. It looked like a Fourth of July celebration reversed. Instead of sending fireworks into the air, they were coming down.

Vicki moved cautiously. The shaking of the earth was not an aftershock. The earthquake simply would not quit. Though it had been less than half an hour, Vicki felt like it had been going on for days. With each meteor, the earth shook even more.

A wild-eyed man rushed at Vicki and screamed. His head was bleeding, and his right arm hung uselessly at his side.

"Kill me!" he shouted over and over.

Vicki knew there were other survivors, but this was the first person she had seen up close.

"I'll help you," Vicki said, putting her hand on his shoulder.

The man jerked backward. His chest was heaving with each labored breath. "They're gone," he said. "All dead. I'm the only one who got out alive!"

"But you're alive," Vicki said. "That's good."

The man ran, tearing at his hair with his good hand. Vicki put a hand to her mouth when she saw where he was going.

"No!" she screamed.

The man stopped at the edge of a crater and looked back. Smoke and flames gushed from the hole. The man gave one last scream and threw himself into the white-hot flames.

Judd peeked over the edge of the gorge. The ground was crumbling. He stepped to a small ledge to get a better look at Taylor Graham. He was on his back at the bottom.

How could anyone hear the prophecies about the wrath of the Lamb, then experience this and not believe in God? Judd thought. He recalled a comedy show shortly after Buck Williams's article had appeared in *Global Community Weekly.* The show featured a cartoon of a cute little lamb. Sappy music played in the background. Suddenly the lamb turned fierce and went on a rampage. The audience had laughed. Judd wondered if the people who had drawn that cartoon were laughing now, or if anyone would ever laugh again.

A red glow engulfed Judd. He heard a jet pass overhead. Judd looked up and realized it wasn't a plane but a fiery meteor. It slammed into the earth.

The second meteor hit near where Judd had been standing and threw molten rock high into the air. If Judd had stayed where he was, he would have melted from the heat.

But he hadn't stayed at the top of the crater. He had thrown himself down its shifting wall and reached Taylor. The man was too big for him to carry, so he tried to awaken him.

Taylor sat up.

"We gotta get you out of here," Judd said.

Taylor looked at the sky and cursed. "It doesn't matter where we go," he said. "We'll never survive this."

"We have to try," Judd said.

Judd helped Taylor climb out the shallow end of the crater. When they made it back to level ground, another shock threw them to the ground. They half crawled, half walked until they made it to what looked like a parking lot of an old elementary school. The building had been flattened.

"What's that up there?" Judd said, pointing to a hill behind the demolished school.

"Must be a lake or some kind of water plant," Taylor said. "Those concrete walls are locks that change the water level."

Judd watched in horror as one of the walls cracked. Water rushed down the slope right toward them.

"Look out!" Taylor shouted as a meteor slammed into the crumpled school building. The rubble caught fire. Judd could feel the intense heat. They ran. Judd looked back and saw the asphalt melting in a wave that was moving toward them. They were no longer running on pavement but on a gooey, melting mess. Then he heard a hissing. The hot water gushed over them and took them both with it.

Judd clung to Taylor with all his might. The water had saved them from a fiery death, but where would it take them now?

Judd went under, then recovered and gasped for air. It was difficult staying above the swells with his cuffed hands. He had lost all control. He was being led by the cascading water.

Then Judd heard a roar. The earth split not far ahead of them, and the water was rushing into the gorge. Judd watched helplessly as they neared the edge.

Before Lionel opened his eyes, he sensed the fire behind him. The heat was intense. The hair on his arms singed, and he buried his head in the dirt. He looked up. The gas explosion must have made the clouds look funny. He tried to move. His body ached, but it didn't feel like any bones were broken. Conrad sat a few feet away, shaking his head and squinting.

"You should have gotten out of there while you had the chance," Lionel said.

"I could say the same for you," Conrad said. "You risked your life for me."

Lionel looked at the car. The wheels were buried. They would never be able to move it by themselves.

A few boys staggered from the rubble. Lionel knew many had been killed in the explosion. Two leaders barked orders and tried to gather the survivors.

"You think we should go with them?" Conrad said.

"I've got another idea," Lionel said.

Lionel and Conrad moved away from the group. When they had gone a few yards, Lionel heard a whirring. The rumbling of the earth still sounded like a freight train, but this was different.

Conrad pointed to the sky. Lionel saw the meteor and fell to the ground. The sphere slammed into the crater where they had been. The car flew in the air and landed on its top, the wheels spinning.

"Glad we didn't stay there," Conrad said.

Lionel looked up. Other meteors streaked through the black and purple clouds, some huge, some only the size of Lionel's hand. The small ones didn't do as much damage but were just as deadly.

"We gotta get under something," Conrad said.

"Not with the earthquake," Lionel said. "Anything we get under is likely to fall on us."

"Then where?" Conrad said.

Lionel scanned the area. What had been flat was now a series of hills and valleys. The main compound building was now a fiery crater. The spot where the leaders had gathered the boys was also a hole in the ground, and Lionel saw bodies a few feet away.

The meteor shower increased. One struck the overturned car. It exploded on impact. The earth continued to roll. Lionel wondered when it would end and if he would still be alive when it was all over.

Ryan was exhausted from digging after only a few minutes. With the weight on his back it was difficult to breathe. He had moved some of the mud and rocks near him, but another rattle had sent boards and plaster falling from above. He was covered in white, chalky dust.

Through a hole in the rubble above he saw clouds. The quake had rolled the roof and upper floors so that he had a clear view of the sky.

The clouds were beautiful. He had never seen anything with such brilliant color. Then he remembered the show he had watched on television about violent storms. Every one of them had weird cloud formations. From the looks of these, Ryan was in for trouble.

He struggled against the slab, but he couldn't move or even feel his legs. He had hoped to be able to move a few inches with all the digging he had done. But he was stuck in the mud and rocks and dust.

He closed his eyes and prayed. Then he thought of his friends. Where were they? What could they be going through? Were they even alive?

He opened his eyes and saw a television remote control floating in the water. The level was rising.

A flash. A thunderous roar. He saw flames streak through the air and wondered if this was some kind of attack. It sounded like the special effects on his video games, but this wasn't a game.

Finally, he understood. This was what Bruce Barnes had written about. Rayford Steele's words came back to him.

" 'The sun became black as sackcloth of hair, and the moon became like blood,' " Rayford had read from Revelation. " 'And the stars of heaven fell to the earth, as a fig tree drops its late figs when it is shaken by a mighty wind. Then the sky receded as a scroll when it is rolled up, and every mountain and island was moved out of its place.' "

Ryan caught a glimpse of more meteors. Since it was morning, he knew he couldn't see the moon. But wherever it was shining, he knew it was as red as blood.

Chaya coughed and choked as the debris settled. She stretched as far as she could but did not find her father. She screamed for him, then prayed.

A flash. Screams in the distance. The ground shuddered.

Chaya had read much of Bruce's writings since his death. She knew other prophecies leading up to the earthquake had been fulfilled. But she was not prepared for this.

Bruce had said the earthquake would touch every place on the globe. There would possibly be volcanic activity as well. As the meteorites hurtled to earth, she recalled what Bruce believed would happen to those who were living at the time of the great earthquake.

"The people of earth will believe God is responsible for all these events," Bruce had written. "And they will cry out to be killed."

Chaya could understand that feeling. Though her belief in God made her want to keep going, others had nothing to believe in. For them, life was hopeless.

She did not see the meteors. When she heard the explosions and smelled the fire, she knew what it was.

Something moved in the rubble. Her father groaned.

"Why?" Mr. Stein cried. "Why don't you kill me now and get it over with!"

Chaya called out for her father, but he continued his ranting. "If you are so good and merciful, why are you doing this to us?" he screamed.

"Do not blame God," Chaya said.

"He has taken my wife," Mr. Stein said. "He has ruined everything I have worked for. Why shouldn't I blame him?"

"God is still calling you to himself," Chaya said. "He is merciful and gracious, even now."

"Mercy and grace are poured out with an earthquake?" Mr. Stein said. "Death and destruction are a display of love?"

"If you turn to God, he will show you mercy," Chaya said.

Chaya listened as her father struggled against the weight of his destroyed home. He was trapped. And the meteors were falling around them.

Darrion couldn't wait any longer. Though the earthquake continued to roll, she bolted out of the shelter and closed the door as tightly as she could. The basement floor was littered with computer parts, storage boxes, and broken canning jars. An oak tree stuck through the kitchen floor above.

Darrion gingerly made her way up the stairs, clinging to the rail as the quake rolled on.

"Mrs. Moore?" Darrion called.

No answer.

The drapes were open in the living room. Considering all the shaking, things looked OK. Then Darrion saw the tiny breakfast nook in the back. She closed her eyes and turned away. Mrs. Moore was still at the breakfast table, her finger curled around a cup of coffee. On top of her was the huge tree. It had flattened her and the heavy wood table.

At least you didn't suffer, Darrion thought.

Darrion couldn't stay. She didn't want to be inside with a dead body. She knew Donny was at the church. She had to tell him. She unlocked the front door and ran outside. The pavement in front was intact. Shards of glass from broken windows littered the lawn. A brick wall of the duplex had collapsed, but Darrion was hopeful. If this was the extent of the damage, others might be alive.

Then she saw the clouds. She heard the meteors before she saw their red glow. She dove under a car as the first one fell to earth.

FOUR

The Aftermath

9:51 A.M.

VICKI could hardly believe the man had killed himself. The Bible was right; others felt the same despair. Vicki wondered what people who had a will to live would do. Who would help them?

In the distance, Vicki saw a hospital. The multistoried parking garage had fallen. Ambulances were upside down or deep in ruts. People ran frantically about looking for family members.

Vicki kept going. She scrambled over a huge stone that had fallen, then realized she was in a graveyard. Headstones lay flat. Unearthed coffins spilled bones and tattered clothes. Vicki carefully picked her way through. When she was almost on the other side, a tremendous shock sent her reeling. She fell into a soft place, then felt withered bones beside her. She was in an open casket!

41

Vicki climbed out. No matter how much she brushed at the dirt, she didn't feel clean again.

She made it over the stones to the other side of the cemetery. She jumped to the ground and stopped. Something was strange. The ground wasn't moving.

She looked up. No clouds. No meteors. The sun reappeared. It was a bright Monday morning.

Vicki fell to the ground on her knees. She felt relieved it was finally over. She felt sadness for Mrs. Jenness and uncertainty for her friends. And she was alone.

Judd and Taylor were swept away with the current. The water carried them back over the route they had walked a few minutes earlier. The pilot held Judd's jacket tightly and tried to stay above the surface. Judd held tightly to Taylor as well.

Judd realized where they were. The collapsed farmhouse had been here. In front of them was the tree, now perched at a weird angle. From one of the limbs, hanging just above the surface of the water, was the tire swing.

"Swim!" Judd yelled.

"What do you mean, swim?" Taylor said. "I can hardly breathe!"

"If we can move a little to the left, we can make it to the tire," Judd said.

Judd and Taylor kicked, but it didn't seem to do any good. The water had a mind of its own. At the last second, the current swirled to the left. Judd managed to reach out and catch the tire with his left hand. Taylor let go of Judd's jacket and grabbed for the swing too. He missed. He grasped Judd's feet and caught one before he was swept away.

Judd held on, then managed to get both arms through the tire. But Taylor was floundering. He couldn't get a good grip on Judd.

"Pull yourself up!" Judd screamed.

"I can't," Taylor yelled back. "Looks like this is it!"

"Don't say that," Judd yelled. "We're gonna get out of this."

Judd tried to wrap his legs around Taylor's chest. Judd looked up and realized they were only a few yards from the chasm.

The ground stopped shaking. The sun came out. Judd heard birds. There were no meteors. Still they had to fight the water.

Judd finally got a good hold on Taylor. He

reached his hand out to pull the man to the tire.

"Almost there," Judd shouted. "You can do it!"

Taylor stretched out his arms. The water was dirty brown as it swirled past him. Chunks of meteor dropped over the edge. If Judd could reach Taylor's hands, the two could stay on the swing until the lake ran dry and the water stopped.

The pilot was almost to safety when a submerged log hit them both. The log hit Judd's legs, and he nearly lost hold of the tire. The log hit Taylor Graham in the face. The man let go and was sucked under in the current.

"No!!!" Judd yelled.

Judd didn't see Taylor until he surfaced at the edge of the chasm. Taylor looked back, blood streaming down his face. He lifted his handcuffs into the air and plunged out of sight.

Judd hung on to the tire. He closed his eyes. They had been so close to making it. Close to life. But close to death as well. The tire swung with the current. Judd put one leg through and then another. He sat there, the water rushing under him.

The sun was out. Everything seemed quiet

and normal. Everything except the earth that had turned inside out.

Conrad and Lionel scooted toward the perimeter of the compound. A chain-link fence lay crumpled on the ground, the metal poles twisted or snapped in two.

Meteors slammed into the soft ground, leaving huge craters. Lionel felt like they were dodging incoming fire from an unseen enemy.

"You think we'll survive this?" Conrad said when they stopped at the base of a tree.

"The Bible says some will," Lionel said.

"What do you mean?" Conrad said.

"It's a long story," Lionel said. "Remind me to tell you when this is over."

"Where are you headed?" Conrad said.

"I have friends in Chicago I need to get back to," Lionel said.

"That's where my brother's stationed," Conrad said. "You want to go together?"

"Sounds like a plan," Lionel said.

The rocking of the earth stopped. The terrible noise was gone. Sunshine hit Lionel in the face. He looked at the blue sky.

"It's like it never happened," Conrad said.

"But it did," Lionel said. "Look at that."

Lionel pointed toward the compound. There was no road. All the buildings were flat. The car Lionel wanted to escape in was on fire. Remains of burning meteors dotted the landscape.

"What do we do now?" Conrad said.

"I'm getting out of here before they catch me," Lionel said.

Then Lionel heard a quick rumbling. A violent shake rattled the earth.

"Aftershock!" Lionel said.

"Look out!" Conrad yelled.

Lionel looked up as the tree they were under crashed down. Lionel dodged the trunk. He thought he was safe until a good-sized limb smacked him in the head. Lionel heard the sickening thud and felt the bark against his skull.

He slumped to the ground and passed out.

Ryan stared at the rising water. He could judge the intensity of the earthquake by the ripples. He still saw the sky through the demolished house. It had been some time since the last meteor.

Light. Glorious light. The sky turned a brilliant blue. He looked at the water. No ripples.

It's over, Ryan thought. *It's really over!*

Ryan put his hands on the muddy floor and pushed up. The water was halfway to his elbows. He couldn't budge the weight that pinned him, but he could raise up enough to see the burst water pipe. He figured it had been about twenty minutes since the pipe burst. Maybe a half hour. Another hour or two and the water would be over his head. He had to either dig out or get help.

Ryan believed the water might help lift whatever was holding him down. If he could keep digging and let the water do its work, there was a chance he could get out.

He used the flashlight until a wooden spoon floated by. Ryan grabbed it and furiously scraped at the mud under his body.

He didn't want to die. He certainly didn't want to survive the great earthquake and then drown. Focusing on the rising water made his heart beat faster, so he talked to himself to calm down.

"If I make it out of here, I'm going straight to the school and find Vicki," Ryan said. "She'll want to know that I'm OK. Then I have to find Darrion."

Ryan did another push up, but he was still trapped.

"OK," he said, "that's the best I can hope

for—get out of here and find Vicki and Darrion. Worst case, I'm stuck. Nobody finds me and I drown."

Ryan paused, then cocked his head.

"That's not without its good points, because then I'd be in heaven with Bruce. I'd get to meet his family. That'd be cool."

Ryan shook his head. "I don't think I'm ready for that," he said. "I want to be here for the Glorious Appearing Bruce talked about. I want to see Jesus coming again."

Something moved above him. A piece of wood fell into the water.

"Hello?" Ryan yelled. "Anybody up there?"

Ryan listened carefully. Someone or something was up there.

"Can you help me?" Ryan said. "I'm stuck! Can anybody hear me?"

Then Ryan heard familiar sounds. Sniffing. Pawing. Phoenix moved around the edges of the rubble. Finally he put his head over the hole and looked down.

"Hey, boy," Ryan said.

Phoenix barked. He wagged his tail and planted his feet like he expected Ryan to chase him.

"Go get help," Ryan said. "Go get somebody!"

Phoenix just looked into the hole.

"OK, so just bark," Ryan yelled. "Come on, bark!!"

Chaya listened as the last of the shifting rubble settled. "It's over, Father," she said.

Mr. Stein furiously tried to pull himself out from under the wreckage, then he stopped. Chaya couldn't even hear him breathe.

"Father?" she said.

Finally he answered. "You are right; it is over," Mr. Stein said. "How can I go on? How can one man lose so much and still want to live?"

"We have each other," Chaya said.

"I have lost everything!" Mr. Stein said. "I have no daughter. You betrayed me. You betrayed your family and your faith."

Chaya shook her head. She couldn't see her father, but she could imagine the look on his face. "We mustn't fight," she said. "We must pull together and try to survive this."

"What does it matter?" Mr. Stein said.

Chaya coughed and groaned.

"What is it?" Mr. Stein said. "Are you hurt?"

"Something happened to my back," Chaya said. "It is difficult to breathe."

Chaya heard her father struggle again, then lay still.

"I wish I could help, but I can't," Mr. Stein said. "Can you move at all?"

"No," Chaya said. "I am like you. Are you injured?"

"Nothing serious," Mr. Stein said.

They were silent for a moment. Then Mr. Stein said, "I suppose you believe there is some great plan in all of this."

"I don't understand it all," Chaya said, "but I do believe God is in control, if that is what you mean."

"I'm sorry I brought it up again," Mr. Stein said. "Let's not talk of those things."

"It is the one thing we should talk about," Chaya said. "It is the most important thing of all."

"You are like your mother."

"Thank you."

"That was not a compliment."

"I know. But I take it as one."

"Your mother tried to convince me to allow you back into the family," Mr. Stein said. "She wanted to forgive you and accept you."

"And you could not."

"Not after what you did," Mr. Stein said. "I suppose that's why she decided to become a foster parent."

"Vicki?"

"Yes."

Chaya wondered if Nicolae High had been damaged as badly as her house. If Vicki had been able to get the *Underground* inside, some kids had probably read it before the quake.

"What did you decide to keep from your mother's belongings?" Mr. Stein said.

Chaya moved on her side and reached in her front pocket. The jewelry was still there. "I kept the gold broach I gave her," Chaya said. "Is that all right?"

"Why did you really come here?" Mr. Stein said, ignoring her question.

"I told you," Chaya said, "I needed something to help me remember her."

"Is that the truth?" Mr. Stein said. "Doesn't your new faith teach it is a sin to lie?"

Chaya bit her lip. "I suppose I did want to see you once more," she said. "But I swear, I lost track of time. I didn't stay on purpose."

"You wanted to see me once more, so you could break my heart."

The two were only a few feet apart, separated by wood and debris. Neither could see the other. Chaya thought it was best this way. Her father could not get up and storm off like he wanted. He was trapped.

"How long do you think it will take until someone finds us?" Chaya said.

"If everyone is in the same shape we are in, there will be no one," Mr. Stein said. He sighed. "I suppose there will be someone who will come along within a day or two."

"A day or two!?" Chaya said.

Chaya coughed. She felt something on her lip and wiped it away. Her hand came away with specks of blood.

Darrion stayed under the car until the meteor shower ended. Soon the earth stopped shaking. Darrion climbed out and surveyed the damage.

Some houses were harder hit than others. A few, like the Moores' home, were damaged but not destroyed. Other buildings were flattened. Darrion saw a few people scurrying, rummaging through the rubble. She heard the screams of trapped victims. She heard a police siren behind her. *At least they have a working squad car*, she thought.

Not wanting to take any chances, she ducked behind a mound of dirt. The officer spoke through an amplifier.

"Stay out of your homes!" the officer said. "Do not return to your homes! If you need help, get to an open area where we can find you!"

Darrion thought of her mother. She was still in the custody of the Global Community. If their facilities were anything like the homes in the area, her mother could be dead.

However, those who might be looking for Darrion and Ryan were busy. Or they were dead themselves. That meant she was free to move about.

She wasn't sure where she was. She hadn't paid attention to street signs when they drove her to the Moores' house. But there were no street signs left anyway. She headed north. She had to find the church and tell Mr. Moore about his wife.

FIVE

Lionel's Problem

12:36 P.M.

VICKI had been walking more than two hours. She thought she was going in the right direction, but it was impossible to tell by the streets. Every familiar house or business left standing stood at odd angles.

People wandered about in a daze. Some had no shoes. Others were bleeding and seemed near death. A few had survived horrible burns from the meteors and had to be carried.

Other survivors were beginning the grisly task of bringing out the dead. Bodies lay covered on mounds of dirt. Vicki felt sorry and wanted to help, but something drew her home. She had to find out about Ryan.

Geysers of water shot up from broken fire hydrants. Animals roamed about, sniffing at the rubble and whimpering. A woman clutching a bloody cloth wept in front of a demolished apartment building.

On a normal Monday, the street Vicki was on would have been packed with traffic. Now the only cars getting through the mess were those with four-wheel drive. A man pulled up beside the weeping woman and hopped out. One side of the vehicle was caved in, and the back window was shattered.

"I'm a doctor, ma'am," the man said. "Can I help you?"

"My baby," the woman wept. "Please help my baby."

The doctor lifted the bloody cloth and winced. "Get in my car and I'll take you to one of the emergency shelters."

The woman stood slowly.

Vicki approached. "Where could I find one of those shelters?" she asked.

"The closest is at Nicolae High," the doctor said. "Take you about twenty minutes on foot." He helped the woman in and closed the door.

"Could I have a ride?" Vicki said.

"I'm not going there," the doctor said. He lowered his voice. "I'm taking this lady's baby to the temporary morgue. It's in the other direction."

The doctor pointed Vicki toward the high school. Vicki looked at the mother as she rode away. She wanted to tell the woman

something to comfort her, but she didn't
know what to say.

What could anyone say at a time like this?

Judd swayed as he clung to the tire. Water
plunged over the falls. Trees, cars, huge
chunks of asphalt, even parts of houses were
swept into the newly formed canyon. Every
few minutes Judd spotted another lifeless
body going over the edge. He wondered if
there was any chance Taylor Graham could
have survived.

By noon the current had slowed. Judd put
one foot down to test whether he could stand.
He decided to wait. One wrong step and he
could fall and be swept over like the others.

Judd wanted to search for Taylor, but he
knew things looked grim. He also knew he
had to change clothes and get out of the
handcuffs. The Global Community was
resourceful. As soon as the reeducation camp
was secure, someone would notice they
hadn't arrived. Judd hoped they would find
the burned-out van and believe he was dead.

He had to find help. Someone he could
trust. He wanted to get back to his friends.
That was his most difficult task. On a normal
day with a car, the trip would take two hours

at most. But without a vehicle and with the destruction of the earthquake, he couldn't imagine it taking any less than two days.

The water was shallow now. He looked back at the collapsed locks. The earthquake had smashed the concrete walls. It looked like a monster had taken a huge bite out of it.

Judd gingerly walked to the edge of the chasm, making sure of his footing. He peered over and was horrified. A new lake had formed, much narrower and brown with dirt. Floating at the top were the mud-caked bodies of the dead. Judd looked for Taylor, but identifying him was impossible.

"Can anybody hear me?" Judd shouted, giving it one last try.

Water trickled nearby. Birds flew overhead. No one answered. The only voice Judd heard was his own, echoing off the chasm walls.

He walked around the hole and went east. He knew the interstate was somewhere in that direction. He tested every new hill he climbed to make sure it would hold his weight. It was like walking through a maze. He would choose one route, then find it led to a gap too wide to cross. He doubled back and went another way.

He found the road where the van had wrecked. He picked along what was left of the highway and found crumpled bits of a mirror. Then he spotted a blackened portion of earth. The earth had swallowed the van but opened again, exposing the charred vehicle. Judd climbed down and stood near the driver's side and looked in.

Dirt filled the van completely. Judd tried to open the door but couldn't. He stuck his hands through the window and pulled at the rocks and clay. Finally he found the charred pistol of the guard. Judd fumbled for the keys on his belt, but there were none. They had melted from the heat of the inferno. Judd would have to find another way to get his handcuffs off.

Judd set off again, stepping over dead animals. He decided to stay close to the road. He would pass someone who could help. In the distance he saw a leaning farmhouse. Someone moved on the front porch. Judd decided to chance it.

"Where am I?" Lionel said when he came to.

"Trauma center," Conrad said. "Looks like a tent, but that's what they call it. That tree did a number on your head."

"Tree?" Lionel said. "Is that what hit me?"

"Yeah, you've been out almost two hours," Conrad said. "So much for you heading north. Looks like you're gonna be here for a while."

"What are you talking about?" Lionel said. "Who are you?"

Conrad looked at him strangely and held up his hand in front of Lionel's face. "How many fingers do you see?" he said.

"Two," Lionel said.

"What's your name?" Conrad said.

Lionel rubbed his head and winced. He shook his head. "I don't know," he said. "I honestly don't know my name."

"Do you remember anything about the last week or two?" Conrad said. "The ride down here, the GC camp, the earthquake?"

Lionel's face lit up. "Yeah, the meteors," he said. "I remember them . . . and the earthquake. The noise. Yeah, that's still with me."

"But you don't remember your name or where you came from?" Conrad said.

"Tell me," Lionel said.

Conrad told Lionel what he knew. Lionel was from Chicago. Lionel had told him he had friends back there, but that his parents and other family had vanished in the disappearances.

"What disappearances?" Lionel said.

Conrad patted him on the shoulder. "Sometimes I wish I could forget all that's happened," Conrad said. "You should feel lucky."

"You said something about the GC," Lionel said. "What's that?"

"Global Community," Conrad said. "Don't you remember why you're down here?"

Lionel closed his eyes. "I do remember the drills. The push-ups and sit-ups and laps if you didn't have your stuff memorized."

Lionel opened his eyes excitedly. " 'The greatest goal of the Global Community and its leader, Nicolae Carpathia, is peace. We will strive together for a world without war and bloodshed.' "

"It's coming back," Conrad said. "The problem is, I didn't think you bought into this stuff."

"What do you mean?" Lionel said.

Conrad stood to leave. "I'm going back to the dorm and see if I can salvage some of your stuff. It might jog your memory if you can see some things you brought with you."

"Wait," Lionel said. "You never told me your name."

Conrad smiled and told him. "Wait here for me," he said.

Lionel glanced around the room at the others. Covered bodies lay in one corner.

"I'm in no shape to move," Lionel said.

"And I wouldn't know where to go if I could."

When Ryan rested on his elbows, the water was up to his neck. When he pushed up with his hands he could breathe easier, but his arms got tired. The water was rising, and it wouldn't be long before his strength gave out.

He had given up on digging himself out. No matter how hard he tried, he couldn't slip out from under the pile. If he was going to make it out alive, he needed help.

The water was cold. He could feel his body going numb. His fingers were already pruny, and he felt a tightness in his chest. He didn't think he was bleeding anywhere, but there was a good possibility of broken bones and internal injuries. All the more reason to get help quickly.

Phoenix was still looking down. Ryan had hoped the dog would bark his head off and alert someone. Instead, Phoenix put his head on his paws and laid down by the hole in the roof. The dog whimpered and whined, but Ryan knew that wouldn't bring people running.

Ryan recalled the old *Lassie* reruns he used

to watch with his father. His dad worked long hours and didn't have much time for Ryan. On the weekends, however, they would sometimes curl up on the couch with a bowl of popcorn and watch old television programs. His dad laughed at the old style of clothes. Ryan loved the way Lassie could always figure out what to do. She saved whoever was injured or trapped. He knew no dog could do all that, but it was still exciting to watch.

"Why don't you do something heroic and lower a rope down here?" Ryan yelled. "Dig a tunnel and let the water out or something."

Phoenix panted and kept his head on his front paws.

Ryan picked up a stick floating nearby and threw it hard at the dog. It bounced harmlessly back into the water. Phoenix raised his head and whined.

"Help!" Ryan shouted. "Somebody help me!"

Chaya and her father talked off and on for two hours. As long as Chaya stayed away from her belief in Jesus, Mr. Stein listened and answered. But when she talked about her faith, Mr. Stein was quiet.

Chaya described her studies at the University of Chicago. Finally, she couldn't resist. "I had the same reaction as you when my friend started talking about the New Testament," she said. "I told him I was a Jew. I didn't want to hear any more. But he kept after me."

"You should have told him to leave you alone," Mr. Stein said.

"I did," Chaya said. "He didn't pester me. I read some of the things he suggested—"

"You turned your back on your family and your faith for a boyfriend?" Mr. Stein said.

"He wasn't my boyfriend," Chaya said. "We never dated. We only talked."

Chaya coughed again. More blood appeared as she wiped her cheek. As the sunlight grew brighter, she was able to see the problem. A splintered piece of wood from the piano had penetrated her back. Her left lung had probably collapsed.

"I don't know how much longer I will have," Chaya said.

"Don't worry," Mr. Stein said. "Someone will come."

"For a long time I was trying to win the argument with my friend," Chaya said. "I tried to prove he was wrong. And to prove it, I had to know what he believed. You understand that, don't you?"

"It makes sense to know your enemy's arguments," Mr. Stein sighed.

"The more I read, the more sense it made," Chaya said. "The questions I always had about my faith were answered. I didn't stop being Jewish; it was as if what Jesus said made me complete."

"I will hear no more," Mr. Stein said.

"When I finally believed in Jesus after the disappearances—"

"I said I will listen to no more!"

"—I wanted to argue with you and prove I was right. But I no longer want to win the argument."

"Stop!"

"I love you, Father," Chaya said. "The point is not about me proving you wrong. The point is God."

Chaya coughed violently and tried to catch her breath. She wondered how much longer she could hold on.

Darrion wished she were on her horse. It would have been easier to ride over the downed trees and mountains of automobiles.

She was unfamiliar with the neighborhood of the church. When she and her mother had stayed in the apartment behind Loretta's house, they hadn't ventured out. Now she felt lost.

Darrion found several survivors who were frantically searching for family members. Some had never heard of New Hope Village Church. Others didn't answer her. A few pointed her in the same direction she was going.

Darrion recognized the name of a restaurant. Vicki had ordered takeout there and said it was only a few blocks from the church. Darrion walked past bodies of people who had tried to hide from the earthquake. They had crawled under chunks of asphalt to protect themselves. Now they were crushed.

Finally, Darrion spied the steeple of the church. She climbed over fallen trees. The parking lot was a crater filled with cars and rocks and jutting concrete. The steeple was the only thing standing. The sanctuary was gone. Beautiful stained glass littered the pavement below. The Sunday school rooms and offices were a pile of bricks and glass and mortar. This was all that was left of New Hope Village Church.

Darrion walked closer and noticed some of the pews still in place. Others were pushed against each other like an accordion. She knew Ryan had been moved from his hideout, and that gave her hope. But what about Mr. Moore?

She scanned what had been the parking lot

but didn't recognize his car. She sat down on a pew and put her face in her hands. When she opened her eyes, she saw a pair of tennis shoes. She knelt and found two thin legs in dark blue jeans. The small body was hidden under the pew. Darrion looked at the left hand. No wedding band! It couldn't be Donny!

She grabbed the man's feet and pulled. Darrion gasped at all the blood. One look and she was sure this was Mr. Moore. Sandy and her husband were together. Together with their child.

Darrion was not comforted by that thought. She felt so alone. Where was her mother? Would she eventually find her body too? Or would she ever see her mother again?

Darrion started crying. Uncontrollable sobs. She ran from the church, falling over debris. She knew Vicki's house was not far away, but her mind was reeling. She had to find her mother. She had to find someone she knew. But she had no idea where to go.

SIX

Shelly's Story

1:22 P.M.

VICKI climbed over the crest of a hill and found what used to be Nicolae High. The gymnasium still stood, but the rest of the school looked like a war zone. Teachers and students ran back and forth, shouting, crying. Rescuers would pull someone from the rubble, crushed and matted with blood, then someone else would call for help and a group would rush to the other end.

What had been a finely manicured football field was now a rolling heap of grass and dirt, mixed with cinders from the surrounding track. The goalposts had moved several yards. One was turned totally upside down. The stands were a heap of twisted metal.

Vicki rushed to see if anyone she knew had made it out alive. In the front, where the flagpole had been, Vicki spotted her friend. She was sitting on the ground, crying, holding her hand over one ear.

Then Shelly noticed Vicki and rushed to hug her. Vicki winced when she saw Shelly's wound. The girl's ear was swollen and bleeding.

"I thought Mrs. Jenness took you away," Shelly said.

"She did," Vicki said and quickly told her story.

Shelly gasped when she heard Mrs. Jenness was dead. "Most of the people in the administration wing made it out," Shelly said. "The vice-principal was in one of the classrooms. They haven't found him yet."

"Any idea how many are still in there?" Vicki said.

"There's no way to tell," Shelly said. "It all happened so fast. I barely made it out the window before the wall caved in."

"Is that how you hurt your ear?" Vicki said.

"A brick hit my head once I was outside," Shelly said. "But I stayed inside a long time."

"What happened?" Vicki said.

"I was trying to save you," Shelly said. "One of the secretaries had me working in Mrs. Jenness's office. I thought if I could find your file and destroy it, the GC might leave you alone."

Vicki put a hand on Shelly's shoulder. "How'd you find out I got caught?" Vicki said.

"Word traveled fast," Shelly said. "I had

the drawer open that held your file when I noticed the watercooler shaking. I didn't know what to make of it. Then I remembered what Mr. Steele preached about."

"I wish I had thought that fast," Vicki said. "Mrs. Jenness might be here right now if I had."

"And you might be in a detention center," Shelly said, "or worse."

Vicki nodded. "I can't help feeling guilty about her," Vicki said.

"From what you said, you did everything you could," Shelly said. "And then some."

"It's not that," Vicki said. "Part of me is glad she's not around to bug us. Isn't that awful?"

"We're both sorry she had to die," Shelly said. "I'm sorry she didn't believe the truth. But you can't *make* people believe."

Vicki asked what had happened when the earthquake hit.

"I hurried back to the main office," Shelly said. "The secretary was going nuts. A basketball coach pulled the fire alarm and got on the loudspeaker. He told everybody to get out of the building. If he hadn't done that, there probably would have been a lot more killed."

"Are there doctors here?" Vicki said. "You should get your ear checked."

"There's a long line," Shelly said. "This is

nothing compared to the people over by the gym."

"I need to get home and find Ryan," Vicki said.

"I'm glad he was there instead of the middle school," Shelly said. "We just heard most of the survivors were on a field trip."

"How awful," Vicki said. She invited Shelly to come with her.

"I need to check on my mom," Shelly said. "She was still asleep when I left this morning. Guess she didn't go to work. I'll try to get to your place later if I can. I hope you find Ryan."

Judd approached the farmhouse warily. He figured anyone who lived this close to the reeducation facility would recognize his uniform. If not, the handcuffs would concern them. He passed a mailbox that was still in its place with the red flag in the "up" position. There was no road next to it.

The farmhouse leaned to the left. On the porch, a woman sat in a green metal chair. Her husband stood behind her. The woman cried. On the lawn next to them a sheet covered a body.

"You can stop right there," the man said. He held up a shotgun.

"I don't mean you any harm," Judd said.

"Doesn't matter what you mean," the man said. "Get down on the ground, hands behind your head."

"I'm handcuffed," Judd said.

"I can see that," the man said, motioning with the gun. Judd thought of running, then he heard a click.

"I just need a change of clothes," Judd said. "I'll pay for it. When I get home I'll—"

"If I were you," the woman interrupted, "I'd do as he says."

Judd dropped to the ground.

"Been expecting some escapes," the man said.

"I didn't escape," Judd said. "I was in transport and our van crashed. I got caught in the flash flood. My friend's dead." Judd looked at the sheet by the porch. "A relative?" he asked.

The man ignored his question. "You must have done something pretty bad," the man said. "This is the highest level facility around here."

"Let's just say I don't get along that well with the Global Community," Judd said.

"Meaning what?" the man said.

"Can I get my face out of the dirt to answer you?" Judd said.

"You're fine where you are."

Judd sighed. "I had some documents that exposed the GC for who they really are," he said.

"Which is what?" the man said.

Judd knew if the man and his wife were in love with Nicolae Carpathia like most of the world, he didn't stand a chance. He decided to simply tell the truth.

"The GC don't like people like me because I believe Jesus is the only person we should serve," Judd said. "That doesn't make the potentate too happy."

The man looked at the woman as Judd kept his head in the dirt. The gun clicked again, then the man knelt and took Judd by the arm.

"Come on," the man said. "Get up."

"I don't understand," Judd said.

"We have to be careful," the man said. "You're safe with us."

Judd couldn't believe the change in the two.

"You ever heard of the Underground Railroad?" the man said.

Judd nodded.

"That's what we have here," the man said. "I'm Hank. This is my wife, Judy."

Judd shook hands with them, the handcuff chain clinking. The woman looked toward the yard. "That's our son," Judy said. "He was in the pump house when the earthquake hit. The walls caved in on him."

"I'm sorry for your loss," Judd said. "How old was he?"

"About your age," Hank said. "He was the first of us to figure out what the disappearances were all about."

Judd listened as the two explained how they discovered the truth. Jesus Christ had returned for his true followers, and they weren't among them. When they found out the GC was jailing believers, the couple felt God wanted them to help some of them escape.

"The problem is our bunker collapsed," Hank said. "We can keep you at the house as long as you'd like, but we can't guarantee you'll be safe. Your best bet is to get as far away from here as you can."

"If you're part of a railroad," Judd said, "there must be others working with you."

"I can give you some names of people and how to find them," Hank said. "We probably have a couple in your area."

The woman stood stiffly. "We won't be using our son's clothes," she said. "Judd might as well have them."

"First things first," the man said. "I'll take him to the barn and get this off."

The man found a hacksaw in the rubble and carefully cut the bands from Judd's wrists. Judd found a pair of jeans and a shirt that fit and grabbed a jacket as well.

"Wish we could offer you a vehicle of some sort," Hank said. "Everything's ruined. Even the tractor."

"You've done more than I could ever ask," Judd said. "Especially at such a difficult time." Judd looked at the body.

"You get back to your friends," Hank said. "We'll be praying for you."

He pointed Judd in the direction of the interstate. "If anything's getting through to Chicago, you'll find it there."

Lionel felt better in the afternoon, but the knot on his head was huge. He still couldn't remember anything about his life before the Global Community camp.

One of the surviving leaders came to him. He assured Lionel his memory would return soon.

"Conrad told me what you did for him," the man said. "I'll admit we've had our eye on you for a while. You're bright. You catch on quick. You could really go far."

"I'm confused," Lionel said. "I can't even remember what I'm doing here."

"Like I said, it'll come back," the man said.

"Bottom line, guys like you are going into society as morale monitors."

"What's that mean?"

"Believe it or not, there are people out there who don't like the agenda of the Global Community. Once your training is complete, you'll be in a position to keep track of them, report them to the authorities, and take action if you have to."

"What kind of action?" Lionel said.

"Approved monitors carry a side arm at all times," the man said, showing Lionel his pistol. "You have to be ready for anything."

Lionel stared at the pistol. Something seemed wrong, but he couldn't figure out what. "Like a cop?" he finally said.

"Sort of," the man said, "but no one knows you're a monitor."

"What kind of people do I look for?"

"Enemies of Nicolae Carpathia," the man said. "Especially the religious people who aren't with Enigma Babylon. They're probably the most dangerous of all."

After the man left, Conrad came in with Lionel's battered suitcase.

"Had to do some digging to find this," Conrad said, "but you've got some interesting stuff in here."

Conrad pulled out clothes and toiletries.

Then came Lionel's Bible and pages of printed material.

"I hope you don't mind me reading it," Conrad said.

"I don't care," Lionel said. He picked up the Bible and leafed through it. "Are you sure this is mine?"

Ryan's arms were tired and his throat parched. He was so thirsty he tried drinking some of the dirty water in the basement. He spat it out.

He pushed up as far as he could a few inches above the waterline. He couldn't rest on his elbows without going under.

Ryan tried to yell, but his voice crackled. His throat was getting sore. Suddenly Phoenix barked.

"That's it, boy," Ryan managed to say. "Keep it up!"

Phoenix moved away but kept barking. A moment later a man stuck his head through the opening.

"Down here," Ryan said. "Get me out! The water's almost over my head!"

The man didn't say anything. He turned quickly and left.

"No!" Ryan said, trying to scream. "Come back! Help!"

Ryan smacked his fist into the mud. His other hand slipped, and he fell face first into the water. He coughed and sputtered as he pushed up. He felt like crying.

Maybe this is it, Ryan thought. *Maybe this is the end.*

A few minutes later Ryan heard Phoenix bark again. A clatter of rubbish sent pieces of tile down. The man peeked over the edge and let down a rope. Another man at the top steadied him, then both climbed down carefully.

"Boy, am I glad you came back," Ryan said.

"Water's getting deep in here," one man said. "Let's get this off his back."

"I don't think you'll be able to move it," Ryan said. "It's had me pinned since—"

The first man easily lifted what Ryan thought was a concrete slab. Ryan couldn't believe it.

"It's not that heavy," the man said. "Now we have to get you out of here."

Mr. Stein didn't say anything for a while. Chaya heard something outside. Mr. Stein screamed for help and struggled under the weight of the debris.

When no one came, Chaya said, "I am growing weaker. I believe I'm bleeding internally."

"Nonsense," Mr. Stein said. "We'll have you out of here soon."

"It will do no good to avoid the truth," Chaya said. "I am prepared to die."

"You are not going to die—"

"Can't you see, Father?" Chaya said. "You're treating this like you have treated my questions about faith. You don't think about it. You can't live that way any longer. You'll have to face the truth."

"You and your theology," Mr. Stein said.

"I used to think theology was something you read about," Chaya said. "It didn't really matter. Now I know that's not true. If God exists and has spoken to us, he deserves to be heard."

"He did speak," Mr. Stein said. "He gave us the law and the prophets."

"Yes, but now he has spoken to us through his Son," Chaya said.

"Jesus," Mr. Stein muttered. "You think he is the answer?"

"What do you think about him?" Chaya said.

"He was a good rabbi. He taught many things about loving your neighbor. But he—"

"How can you call a man good who says he is God?" Chaya said.

"I don't believe he said that," Mr. Stein said. "His followers wanted to believe he was God."

"If so, why did the disciples give up their lives for a lie?" Chaya said.

Mr. Stein protested, but Chaya wouldn't stop. She began in the Old Testament and described the prophecies of the Messiah. She couldn't tell whether her father was listening or not. But Chaya had the growing feeling that this was her last chance to reach him.

Darrion couldn't think straight. She had seen so much death and so many suffering people. She ran from Donny Moore's body. She wanted to be with the living, not the dead. She wanted to be with her mother or her friends.

She spotted some sort of ambulance slowly making its way through the ruins. She ran to it and caught the attention of the driver.

"Can you help me?" she yelled.

"Are you hurt?" the man said.

"Not really," Darrion said. "I'm looking for my mother."

"This vehicle is only for the injured," the

man said. "Don't look for your mom by yourself, though. The houses are too dangerous to go in. Get to one of the survival posts, and they'll help you."

"Can't you use your radio?" Darrion said.

"Sorry," the man said. "Nearest place you'll find is about a half mile in that direction."

Darrion watched as the van lumbered off. She set out for the survival post and wondered if she would ever see anyone she knew again.

SEVEN

Helping Pete

2:13 P.M.

VICKI finally got her bearings and found the house on her corner, but she realized the ground had shifted so drastically that it was on the other side of the street. Other houses leaned or were destroyed. The end of the house had been blasted by a meteor. It was on fire.

A dog barked. *Phoenix*, she thought. She ran toward him, and the dog jumped on her and nearly knocked her over.

"Where's Ryan?" Vicki said. "Take me to Ryan."

Phoenix bounded over to the rubble that was her house. Vicki climbed onto the roof, which was now at ground level. Phoenix stood next to a hole. Vicki peered down and saw the water-filled basement. She called for Ryan, but there was no answer.

"Is he in there, boy?" Vicki said.

Phoenix barked.

Vicki saw the tree that was now in her kitchen. If Ryan had been there, he was dead.

He's a tough kid, Vicki thought. *He knows how to take care of himself.*

Vicki wanted to go into the basement, but she needed a rope. She raced from the house, but everyone she found was busy with their own rescue efforts. She finally found a long electrical cord she thought would hold her weight.

As she made her way back to the house she spotted a group of people in uniform. Two Global Community guards directed the homeless to shelters. Vicki walked briskly away but stopped when she saw a girl who looked familiar. Her clothes were in tatters, but Vicki recognized Darrion Stahley. Darrion was headed straight for the GC officials.

Vicki hurried to catch up, but Darrion made it first. Vicki feared the men would recognize Darrion's face.

"I have to know about my mother," Darrion said.

"Stand over there and wait," one guard said.

"You don't understand," Darrion said. "Do you know who I am?"

Vicki grabbed Darrion by the arm and turned her around. Darrion hugged Vicki.

"I'll take care of her now," Vicki said to the GC guards.

"Wait, come back here," one guard said.

Vicki wanted to run. Then she saw their guns. They might shoot to kill if they got suspicious.

"Is there a problem?" Vicki said as the guard approached.

"There is if you plan on going back into that subdivision," the guard said.

"I was," Vicki said. "I think my friend's trapped in there."

"Which house?" the guard said.

Vicki pointed.

"There's nobody alive in there," the guard said. "If they did survive the quake, the water's gotten to them by now."

"What are we supposed to do?" Vicki said.

"We've set up temporary shelters for the less injured," the guard said. He pointed toward a tent in what used to be a park. "You and your friend go there now."

"Where did they take the serious cases?" Vicki said.

"Some went to the high school," the guard said. "They airlifted a few others."

Vicki thanked the man, and the two walked to the tent. Instead of going inside, they circled around the back and kept going toward Vicki's house.

"What were you doing?" Vicki said when they were a safe distance away.

"I have to find my mom," Darrion said. "I'm afraid she's dead."

"She might be," Vicki said, "but you won't find her by going to the GC."

"I didn't know what to do," Darrion said. "I saw all those dead people. Mrs. Moore. Donny too. I panicked."

"The Moores are dead?" Vicki said.

Darrion explained what had happened.

"OK," Vicki said, trying to calm her. "I promise we'll find out about your mom. First we need to see if we can find Ryan. I need your help."

As Vicki led Darrion back to her house, she explained what had happened to her. Darrion could only shake her head when she heard about Mrs. Jenness.

Vicki tied the orange electrical cord to the tree that had crashed into their house. A piece of rope was tied to the tree but cut off at the knot. She kept working.

Vicki dangled the cord into the hole and carefully climbed down. Darrion helped steady her. Vicki looked at what had been her home. She could make out the upstairs bedrooms, but the rest was smashed.

While Vicki explored the basement,

Darrion retrieved as many clothes from the bedrooms as she could find.

A few minutes later, Vicki and Darrion sat on a downed tree limb.

"This is where the kitchen was when I left this morning," Vicki said. "Now there's a tree where the table used to be, and we're looking into what's left of the upstairs bathroom."

"Unbelievable," Darrion said.

A vehicle moved between the houses.

"Get down," Vicki said.

Someone was talking over a loudspeaker. "Stay out of your homes! By order of the Global Community, you must not return! If you need help, get to an open area. Looters will be shot!"

Darrion looked at Vicki. "If they catch us with these clothes, how do we prove they're yours?" Darrion said.

"Just stay down," Vicki said.

The vehicle passed. Vicki breathed a sigh of relief. Something moved toward them. Before Vicki could stop her, Darrion stood.

"Hey, you!" someone shouted.

Judd couldn't remember how long the van had traveled from the interstate. They had gone at least a few miles before the earthquake hit. He tried to follow what was left of the two-lane road.

He passed collapsed buildings with farm machinery sunken into the ground. The outer walls of a post office had collapsed, leaving the inside counter standing and a mountain of mail behind it.

Judd kept moving. In the distance he saw the remnants of a collapsed bridge leading to the interstate. He was horrified to find cars underneath, smashed flat by the concrete.

Other motorists worked to rescue those trapped. They pulled bodies from an over-turned bus. Judd walked around the mayhem through a nearby field. Black smoke rose from craters. He followed a drainage ditch through tall weeds until he heard a strange squeaking. He found a motorcycle, upside down. Its front wheel turned slowly.

A few yards away, Judd found the body of a man wearing a black helmet. Judd bent over the man and felt his neck for a pulse.

The man opened his eyes and screamed. Judd jumped back.

"It's OK," Judd said, "I'm here to help."

"I can't move," the biker said. "I've been laying here since this morning, yelling and screaming for someone to hear me." The biker tried to sit up. "Have you seen my bike?"

"It's right over there," Judd said. He knew

enough about such injuries to leave the man alone. He didn't want to move him and make things worse.

"I saw the bridge breaking up and tried to stop," the biker said. "A slab of road rose up like a ramp, and I went flying through the air like one of those daredevils."

"Stay here and I'll get someone," Judd said.

Judd found a man who said he had a stretcher they could use to strap the biker down. It would take a few minutes to free it up. Judd went back to stay with the biker.

"Help's on its way," Judd said. "What's your name?"

"Pete Davidson," the man said, putting out his hand.

Judd shook it and told him his name.

"Where are you headed?"

"Back to Chicago," Judd said. "I have friends I need to check on."

"Why don't you use my bike?"

"I couldn't do that," Judd said.

"It's not that hard to handle," he said.

"It's not that," Judd said. "It's yours. I couldn't take it."

"Look at me," Pete said. "You think I'm gonna be riding anytime soon?"

Judd smiled. "You'll be up and around in

no time," he said. "Besides, we don't even know if it'll still run."

"Put it on its wheels and try," Pete said.

Judd spent a few minutes trying to get the motorcycle right side up. He noticed a huge dent in the gas tank. It was bad, but the tank hadn't ruptured. The cap on the tank was off, and the fuel had emptied onto the ground. Judd rolled the bike close so the man could see it.

"You'll have to make sure you have gas, then plug the hole so it doesn't slosh out. I can't guarantee it'll start, but if it does, you're in business."

"Like I said—"

"Listen to me," Pete said. "You know what happened to the bridge back there. You know every bridge from here back to Chicago is probably in the same shape. Nothing's getting through except some four-wheel drives and bikes like this. You helped me. I help you. Simple as that."

"All right," Judd said, "but you have to do me two favors."

"Name 'em."

"Give me your address so I can return it," Judd said.

Pete gave Judd the information. "What's the other favor?" he said.

"I want to tell you why I helped you," Judd said.

Lionel looked through the papers Conrad had given him and saw notes in the Bible. Still, nothing clicked.

"Does this mean anything to you?" Conrad said.

Lionel read the inscription in the front of the Bible. "To Lionel, from Ryan."

"No," Lionel said. "I don't remember any Ryan."

"You need to get to Chicago and find these people," Conrad said.

"What for?" Lionel said.

"They were your friends," Conrad said. "They know who you are. And they probably know all about this Bible stuff."

"I'm not sure I want to know," Lionel said. "I mean, if it comes back to me, fine. But I can't turn my back on what the Global Community is offering."

Conrad frowned. "You ought to at least give it a chance," he said.

"I'll think about it," Lionel said.

Ryan lay in a furniture store that had been turned into a makeshift hospital. His head was pounding. He felt cold.

He couldn't believe how easily the man had lifted the thing off his back. They had pulled him up from the hole by placing a rope under his arms. Ryan had passed out and woke up at the emergency shelter. He hadn't been able to thank his rescuers.

People around him seemed in worse shape. Some had lost arms or legs. Others wore bandages over their faces.

A woman came and took his temperature. "You're burning up," she said.

"I feel the opposite," Ryan said. "Can I have another blanket?"

The woman brought him some medicine and a drink to wash it down.

Ryan hesitated.

"What's wrong?" the woman said.

Ryan blushed. "I can't take these," he said. "I never learned how to swallow pills like this."

The woman sat on his bed. "You mean you were able to survive the biggest earthquake in the history of the world," she said, "and you're not able to swallow a couple of pills?"

She smiled, pulled the capsules apart, and dropped the contents into the glass of water.

Ryan thanked her.

"See if you can get some rest," the woman said.

"Wait," Ryan said. "How bad is it?"

The woman smiled again. "The doctor will be by as soon as he can," she said. "Rest."

Ryan pulled the covers up and shook.

Someone cleared her throat nearby. "Here," an old woman in the next bed said. She handed him one of her covers.

"You don't have to," Ryan said.

"Can't keep these old bones warm anyway," the woman said. "You look like you can use it."

The woman was too weak to throw the cover to him. She handed it as far as she could, then let it fall to the floor.

Ryan was able to pick it up but couldn't spread it over himself very well. Finally he spoke to the old woman.

"Do you know what's wrong with me?" Ryan said.

"Doctor saw you earlier," she said. "Said something about a wound on your back and a possible infection. Plus some other things."

"What other things?" Ryan said.

"I think he ought to tell you," the old woman said.

Ryan persisted.

The woman held up her hand. "I'm tired," she whispered. "We'll talk when I wake up."

Ryan listened to the woman's labored breathing. *What could be wrong with me?* he thought.

Though her father was silent, Chaya continued giving Scripture after Scripture that showed
Jesus was the true Messiah of the Jews. He had
been rejected by his own people and had been
killed just as Isaiah had prophesied.

"You sound like the rabbi on television,"
Mr. Stein finally said after a few minutes. "He
had an excellent grasp on the Scriptures, but
he was misguided with his conclusion."

Chaya frowned. Vicki said she had been at
Chaya's home when Dr. Tsion Ben-Judah
proclaimed Jesus as Messiah on an international broadcast. Mr. Stein had been angry.

"Then you do not see anything of merit in
what I say?" Chaya said.

"It has nothing to do with merit," Mr.
Stein said. "I will not turn my back on my
faith as you have."

"What would it take for you to believe?"
Chaya said.

Mr. Stein laughed. "I suppose if God
himself were to hold me down and tell me
Jesus was the way, I would believe."

Chaya coughed violently, then regained her
composure. "Isn't that what has happened to
you today?" Chaya said. "God has put you in
a position to hear the truth. You would have
run if all this weren't on top of you."

"I am not afraid of the truth—"

"Then hear it and believe," Chaya said. "God is giving you one more chance to respond to his gift."

"This is a gift?" Mr. Stein yelled. "To have my wife taken from me and now my house and all my possessions destroyed?"

"God gave his only Son for you," Chaya said. "Just as the lamb was slain and its blood put on the doorposts during the Passover, so Jesus died for you and me so we would not have to die. That is the gift of God."

Chaya felt light-headed. Before her father said anything more, she passed out.

EIGHT

Ryan's Bad News

4:08 P.M.

VICKI knew there was no use running. They were caught. When the man came over the rubble, she was surprised to see he had no uniform.

"What are you two doing here?" the man said.

"I live here," Vicki said. "At least, I used to."

"Can you prove it?" the man said.

Vicki thought a moment. She couldn't. At least not with any papers or a driver's license. She shook her head. "I don't have an ID, but this really is my house. Those are my clothes over there."

"If it's really your house," the man said, "you'll know who we found here a few hours ago."

"You found Ryan?" Vicki said.

The man smiled. "He was right down there," he said. "We pulled him out just before the water got to him."

"Is he all right?" Vicki said.

"He was alive," the man said, "but he didn't look good. He'd been trapped the whole day."

"Where is he now?" Vicki said.

"Don't know," the man said. "I helped put him into one of those Ambu-Vans. They took him to get help, but I don't know where."

Vicki thanked the man. She located her purse, then grabbed a few changes of clothes and stuffed them into an overnight bag she found floating by. The water was at ground level.

As Judd waited for the stretcher for Pete Davidson, he told his story of being on an airplane during the disappearances. Judd asked Pete if he could remember where he was that night.

"I'll never forget it," Pete said. "I was at a cycle convention. People come from all over the country. You see a lot of cool machines. I go because it lets me get in touch with old friends. We drink a little.

"Anyway, there's always a few groups of these Jesus bikers. Some guys don't care for 'em. They pretty much leave me alone. I was leaving a bar late that first night when a big group rode in. I knew from the crosses on their jackets that this was one of those Jesus groups.

"I got on my bike and started it up just as they were passing. Then there was this awful noise. I turned around and saw empty bikes going fifty or sixty miles an hour. There were a couple of people still in the group, but most of them had disappeared, like they'd been beamed up somewhere.

"The first bike went down, then the rest followed. There must have been thirty hogs all over the road, twisted up, some of them burning."

"Hogs?" Judd said.

"A type of motorcycle," Pete said. "The best you can buy, as far as I'm concerned. Anyway, we only found a couple of bodies. There were leather jackets spread out on the road. Boots. Rings and chains."

"What did you do after that?" Judd said.

"I went back into the bar," Pete said. "I was too shook up to drive."

"Do you have any idea what happened that night?" Judd said.

"I've heard some theories," Pete said. "Space aliens took them. They rode into another dimension. That kinda thing. Never heard anything that made sense to me."

"Did you ever actually talk with anyone from that group?" Judd said.

"Never let them get that close," Pete said.

Judd explained what had happened to his family. They had vanished too. "The interesting thing is," Judd said, "everybody I know who disappeared claimed they had a relationship with Jesus."

"Same here," Pete said. "My mother always went to church. Said she prayed for me every day. I found her clothes in a rocking chair in her living room when I went to her house."

"That's the key to understanding the vanishings," Judd said. "It wasn't just people who went to church or were religious that got taken; it was people who knew Jesus as their Savior."

"What's that mean?" Pete said.

Judd explained the gospel. "God created people to have a relationship with him, but people sinned. Since God is holy, he can't tolerate sin. When the time was right, Jesus came into the world and lived a perfect life. Then he died in our place and rose from the dead. Now, if people ask for forgiveness, Jesus comes into their life and God forgives them."

Pete put his head back and looked into the sky. "I saw this magazine article that talked about that," he said, "but I wasn't sure it was right."

"Do you admit that you've done wrong things?" Judd said.

"Yeah, plenty."

"Do you want God to forgive you?"

"If he can," Pete said.

"He can and he will," Judd said. "The Bible says if you confess your sins, God is faithful and will forgive you."

Pete stroked his beard. "My mom used to try to tell me this stuff, but I wouldn't listen."

"Now's the perfect time," Judd said.

"How would I do something like . . . what you're saying?" he said.

"Pray with me," Judd said. "God, I'm sorry I've sinned, and I ask you right now to forgive me."

Pete closed his eyes and whispered the words as Judd spoke.

"I believe Jesus died for me and that he rose from the dead," Judd continued. "Come into my heart now and save me. Amen."

Pete smiled. "If I hadn't hit that incline, or if you hadn't come this way, I'd never have prayed like that."

"God loves you, Pete," Judd said. "I'm just glad I found you."

Before the man with the stretcher returned, Judd tried to start the motorcycle again. There was enough gas in the tank to get the engine going, but as hard as Judd tried, it wouldn't start.

"You're kicking it hard enough," Pete said. "It just sounds like something's wrong with the engine. The bike took a pretty bad hit."

The man put the stretcher under Pete and secured him tightly. Pete motioned for Judd.

"If you can't get my bike going, you could go back to my place," Pete said. "I have a dirt bike, which might be better for you. Between here and Chicago you'll be able to use something that'll climb."

"Where's your house?" Judd said.

"Next exit south," Pete said. "About three miles or so."

Judd looked at the highway. No cars moved on the broken road, but he hoped someone with a four-wheel drive would come by soon heading for Chicago.

"I don't want to go the other way if I don't have to," Judd said. "Besides, we don't know if your other bike survived the quake."

Pete looked away and rubbed his eyes.

"What is it?" Judd said.

"My girlfriend," Pete said. "I was heading back to my house this morning. I was hoping you'd go back for the bike and check in on her. Maybe you could tell her what you just told me. You know, about the Jesus thing. Then you could tell her where I am."

Judd smiled. He got the directions to Pete's house and helped the man load Pete onto the back of a four-wheel drive truck.

"You'll go then?" Pete said.

"I'm on my way," Judd said.

Pete smiled. "I guess my mom's prayers worked after all," he said.

Lionel thanked the doctor, and Conrad came into the room.

"What did he say?" Conrad said.

"Not much," Lionel said. "Other than this knot on my head and the memory loss, I'm fine."

"How long are you gonna be here?"

"As long as it takes," Lionel said. Then he lowered his voice. "But the doctor says there's no reason I can't jump right back in as long as I don't suffer any side effects."

Conrad pulled out a page from Lionel's belongings. "There's stuff in here about a Jewish rabbi who became a Christian," he said. "Interesting. I always thought Christians were people who put their brains on the shelf."

"Honestly, I can't remember anything about it," Lionel said.

"This rabbi says everything that's

happened was predicted in the Bible,"
Conrad said. "Do you think there's any way
to find these friends of yours?"

"I don't see how," Lionel said. "I don't
have names, addresses, phone numbers, and
even if we did, the earthquake's destroyed
communication lines."

"True," Conrad said, "but we just had a
briefing from one of the top guys. He says
the Global Community is already rebuilding
an international communications network.
Before the quake, the GC bought up all of
the satellite and cellular communication
companies."

"But it'll take months to get that back up
and running," Lionel said.

"Take a look," Conrad said. He pulled
back a flap of the tent. Lionel shaded his face
with a hand. A few hundred yards away,
workers pushed a cellular tower in place.

"Already?" Lionel said.

"I guess being able to talk with people is
more important than saving lives," Conrad
said. "Don't tell anybody I said that."

"That doesn't make sense," Lionel said.
"Nicolae Carpathia is a man of peace. The
Global Community cares for people, right?"

"I don't want to get in trouble," Conrad
said, "but from what I heard from my
brother, Carpathia wants power. Control.

He's bought the media. He controls the countries with the most oil reserves. Now he's in control of all the phone and communication lines. He owns and controls everything and everybody."

"But that's good, right?" Lionel said. "If somebody we can trust is in control of all that, there won't be any more wars."

Conrad frowned. "I don't know what to believe," he said. "But I want to check out what this rabbi is saying."

Lionel felt an uneasiness in his gut. Something was wrong, but he didn't know what. Since he had awakened from his injury, he felt there was more than his memory missing. It felt like a hole in his soul. He tried hard to remember. Was it something he was supposed to be doing? Was he letting someone down? He felt guilty for not remembering. He touched the knot on his head and winced. A big part of his life *was* missing, and he had a feeling he was never going to find it again.

Ryan awoke without pain. He wanted to get up and walk out of the converted furniture store and find the others, but he couldn't move. He thought they might have him strapped down.

He turned to the woman in the next bed. She was staring at him.

"I'm glad you're up," Ryan said. "I really want to know what's wrong with me. I can't wait for the doctor. Will you tell me?"

The woman didn't answer.

"Before you say no," Ryan continued, "just hear me out. I have these friends I've been living with since the disappearances. My mom and dad were killed, so I've been staying with them. Maybe you'll get to meet them. Anyway, I was thinking if I knew what was wrong, they could come get me and take care of me until I get better."

The woman just stared at him.

"Please," Ryan said, "what did you hear the doctor say?"

The woman didn't move. Didn't bat an eye. She seemed stuck in the same position.

"Ma'am?" Ryan said. Then he said it a little louder. The third time he screamed and a nurse came. She bent over the woman, then pulled the sheet over her head.

"She can't be dead," Ryan said. "She was talking to me just a little bit ago."

"Go back to sleep," the nurse said. "There's nothing you can do."

"Tell me what's wrong with me," Ryan said. "She said the doctor was checking me for an infection in my back. Is that true?"

The nurse hesitated, then sat on his bed. "I'll tell you what I know, though I'm not supposed to," she said.

Ryan nodded and said, "Thank you."

"There is a possible infection in a wound in your back," she said. "Something about a cut back there and the water being dirty. But that's not really the big problem."

"What is?" Ryan said.

"Do you know what *paralysis* means?"

"Yeah, like paralyzed, you can't move, right?"

"That's right."

"Well, that's not what I have," Ryan said. "See, I can move my arms anywhere I want."

"Something happened during the earthquake," the nurse said. "Either you fell on something or something fell on you. It injured the nerves in your back that make your legs work."

"Am I going to die?" Ryan said.

The nurse looked away. Ryan remembered when he was a kid getting his appendix removed. He had asked the doctor then if he was going to die. The doctor laughed and smiled at him. He wanted the nurse to do the same now, but she didn't. She looked back with tears in her eyes.

"I'm not supposed to tell you any of this,"

she said. "But there are so many patients, and the few doctors we have can't keep up with everybody."

"It's OK," Ryan said. "I'm not afraid to die. I just don't feel that bad."

"Can I get you anything?" she said.

"Yeah, you can get word to my friends," Ryan said. "They'll be upset if they don't know what happened to me."

"Are you sure your friends are . . ."

"They're OK," Ryan said. Then, for the first time, he seriously considered whether he was the only one who had survived the wrath of the Lamb earthquake. He pushed the thought from his mind.

"Why don't I get you a pen and some paper," the nurse said. "Writing something down to them might be the best thing in case . . ."

"In case what?" Ryan said.

"I think it would just be a quicker way to get them a message, that's all," the nurse said.

"Sure," Ryan said.

Mr. Stein was calling Chaya's name when she awoke. She tried to speak but couldn't. Finally she choked out, "I am here."

"What happened?" Mr. Stein said. "Are you all right?"

"No, I am not all right," she said. "I told you, I am hurt. I am bleeding."

Mr. Stein tried again to lift the weight from his back. The more he struggled, the more the weight shifted onto him.

"I can't get to you," Mr. Stein said.

Chaya thought of Jesus and his teachings. She knew the power of his stories. They came from daily life. The disciples could relate to the tiny mustard seed. They knew what wheat and tares were. Then Chaya thought of her own situation. She and her father were buried under a mountain of rubble. *This*, she thought, *is a perfect example*.

Chaya took a breath. "Father, you are trapped," she said. "You are helpless to save yourself. Someone from outside must come and give us assistance."

"That is why I have been yelling since this morning," Mr. Stein said.

"It is the same with your spiritual life," Chaya said. "No matter how many good things you try to do, or how much you try to follow the law, you know in your heart that there is sin."

Mr. Stein was silent.

"Only God can forgive sins, and that is what Jesus came to do," Chaya said. "He was the perfect sacrifice. When we were dead in our sins, Messiah died for us."

"You are delirious," Mr. Stein said.

"I am telling you the truth," Chaya said. "Jesus said he was the way, the truth, and the life. You can only come to God the Father through him. Please receive him now before it is too late."

Chaya felt a burning in her chest, and her breathing was getting more difficult. The dust had settled around her in a white film. Each breath sent a tiny white puff into the air.

She listened for her father's response. He was past the point of struggling against the weight. She knew he had resigned himself to wait for help. But she couldn't tell whether this last thought had gotten through to him.

NINE

Chaya's Last Chance

5:52 P.M.

VICKI wanted to find Ryan, but she knew they needed shelter for the night. The sun was going down, and it was getting colder. Vicki and Darrion backtracked to the high school.

She asked about Ryan, and a man with a clipboard looked through several pages. He shook his head. "No Ryan Daley here," he said, "but we've got a bunch of victims who haven't been identified yet."

"Where are they?" Vicki said.

The man pointed to a corner of the gym where bodies lay covered.

"A doctor told me you didn't have a morgue here," Vicki said.

"We didn't a few hours ago," the man said.

"Don't you have any unidentified injured?" Vicki said.

The man looked at his clipboard again. "We do, but there's no one who fits the

111

description of your friend," he said. "You can look if you'd like."

Vicki and Darrion were led into the locker room. A few mattresses lay on the floor. Some people moaned and cried with severe injuries. The shower had been turned into an operating room. It was clear from a quick look that Ryan wasn't there.

Darrion looked nervously at Vicki. "You think we should look in the gym?" she said.

"He's not dead," Vicki said. "Come on, I'll prove it."

Vicki lifted sheet after sheet from the dead bodies. Ryan wasn't there. As they were leaving, Shelly returned. Vicki could tell she had been crying.

"I made it back to our trailer," Shelly said, "but the whole place was destroyed. Trailers on top of each other, twisted, broken in two."

"What about your mom?" Vicki said.

Shelly shook her head. "I found our neighbor next door who got out," she said. "The ground opened up and swallowed my house whole. I assume my mom was still inside, but there's no way to tell."

Vicki hugged Shelly. "Come on, you're with us now," Vicki said.

The next shelter was a mile away. Vicki was told there were injured being treated there and beds for those who needed a place to sleep.

"I can't believe the house is gone," Vicki said. "I wonder if Judd's place is still standing."

"I saw Mark before I got to the high school," Shelly said. "He and his aunt made it, but they can't stay in the house. He did have some good news, though."

"What's that?" Vicki said.

"He said he saw Buck Williams driving his Range Rover near the church," Shelly said. "At least Buck made it."

"But what about Chloe and Loretta?" Vicki said. "And Tsion Ben-Judah?"

Shelly shook her head. "Mark only saw Buck."

Judd rode with Pete a few minutes on the back of the truck, then walked to the exit Pete had described. The exit sign was facedown.

Judd had to climb down a culvert and cross some twisted railroad tracks. He climbed up the other side and followed Pete's directions. A few minutes later he came to a creek. He crossed it and found the road Pete had described. He found several leveled houses.

Pete's house was a small, white ranch. It had a separate garage in the back. Judd went to the house and managed to crawl into the kitchen through a window. The ceiling had collapsed but was still a few feet off the floor. Judd had forgotten to ask the girl's name, so he called out, "Hello?"

Judd's voice echoed in the rubble. No one answered. Judd crawled through the kitchen. He saw no sign of the girl. A ray of light came from a utility area.

He saw the woman's hands first. She had been doing laundry when the quake occurred. Or perhaps she had run in there for safety. Judd felt for a pulse, but he knew there was no use. Her skin was chalky white and cold. He could barely make out her face in the midst of the wood and plaster.

Judd couldn't find a way out, so he retraced his steps to the kitchen. The refrigerator had toppled but was still closed. If he was going to drive to Chicago, he would need some food. He grabbed a loaf of bread and a package of ham that was still cool in the fridge. He found a jug of bottled water and stuffed a few other things into a garbage bag he found under the sink.

The garage was crumpled. He finally got the door open but saw there was nothing inside that could be saved. The quake had tossed old lawn mowers and tillers onto motorcycles. The dirt bike wasn't there. In the grass behind the garage, Judd found it. He figured someone had used it, then propped it against the garage before the quake had hit.

He jumped on and tried to start it. The bike sputtered a few times, then the engine took off with a deafening sound. He opened the gas cap and rocked the bike. Half full.

As Judd tied his provisions onto the seat, he saw someone in the distance waving and running toward him. Would they believe him if he said Pete had given him permission? Judd decided not to chance it. He roared away and followed the creek until he came to the main road.

Judd wanted to tell Pete about his girl-friend, but the light was fading and he had a long way to go. He decided to wait until he returned the bike to tell Pete.

He clattered around the bridge, still littered with survivors and the dead. Where other vehicles couldn't go, Judd plowed through. In some areas, Judd had to get off and walk. As the sun faded, Judd looked for the headlight and was surprised the bike had none.

Guess I won't be driving all the way home tonight, Judd thought.

Judd came to a stop at the edge of the Des Plaines River. The top of the bridge stuck out of the rushing water. Judd stood on the bank and looked across. Unless he could find a raft or some other way across, he was stuck.

Judd rode east into a wooded area. He dodged uprooted trees and stumps until he came to a cliff overlooking the river. Judd stopped the motorcycle and leaned it against a tree. It was peaceful here. Squirrels played in the fallen trees. Birds sang. It was a perfect day, except for the fact that the earth had shaken itself so violently that morning.

Farther east the river narrowed. A dam still stood. If Judd could get to it, there was a chance he could drive a few more miles before dark.

He turned to retrieve the motorcycle but stopped dead in his tracks. Three men stood around the bike silently watching Judd.

Lionel ate a small dinner and looked through his belongings. He closed his eyes and tried to remember. The ID card in his wallet showed his name and his picture and said he was a freshman at Nicolae Carpathia High School in Mount Prospect, Illinois. Lionel turned the card over and over.

He picked up a spiral notebook and leafed through it. It was a journal of sorts. Random thoughts and verses written out. Notes on sermons he had heard. Lionel found names. Judd. Ryan. Vicki. Bruce. Something had happened to Bruce. Lionel had taken it hard.

"I don't know what we're going to do without him," Lionel read. "He was more than just a teacher, he was our friend."

Lionel also found references to something called the "Trib Force." He closed the book and laid back. The words made no sense. He couldn't deny the journal was his.

Lionel's superior walked in. He pulled a chair close to the bed and sat.

"How are you feeling?" the man said.

"As good as I can be," Lionel said. "Ready to go, I guess."

"Good," the man said. "We've been meeting this afternoon. The top brass feels this is the perfect time to put our monitors in place. The earthquake has changed everything. If you'll agree, we'll put things in motion and get you transferred to a monitor station as soon as transportation is open."

"Monitor station?" Lionel said.

"The program is just getting started," the man said. "Each location will have two monitors. You'll report to a regional commander in your district. They'll report to us, and we report directly to Global Community Command."

"So I'll go with somebody else?" Lionel said.

"You can suggest someone if you want," the man said. "I would expect to have you out of here within the week if you agree."

Lionel felt the bump on his head. "A lot's happened since I got here," he said. "I've been reading things I wrote and trying to figure out who I am."

"It'll come back to you—just give it time."

"Would it be OK if I slept on it and told you in the morning?" Lionel said.

"Sure," the man said. "You think about it."

The nurse brought Ryan a pen and paper and left him alone. Ryan stared at the blank page. He felt hot. Beads of sweat popped out on his forehead. He wiped them away and tried to prop himself up, but again, he couldn't move. Someone came to take the dead woman away. Ryan bunched up the covers enough to put the pad of paper in the right position.

He wrote down Vicki's address and gave the location of New Hope Village Church. Someone would get the message to Vicki.

I'm writing this to you, Vicki, but I'm hoping you'll be in touch with Judd and Lionel as well.

First, I shouldn't have been surprised at what happened because this was everything Bruce said. The wrath of the Lamb and all. We can be glad God keeps his promises, I guess. The nurse said I should write to you. I never was a letter writer, but she thought it was a good idea.

Ryan laid back and rested. His arm was already tired from trying to hold the pad in the right position. He had to shake the pen so the ink would come out. He continued.

You've been like a big sister to me. I never had one. Judd was a big brother, and Lionel was a good friend. I hope I wasn't too much of a pain to have around.

I guess there's a chance I could get up and walk out of here, but it doesn't look good. So I want to tell you all to hang in there. God didn't let us survive this long without there being a reason. No matter where you go or what happens, I want you to remember how much you mean to me. I can't thank you enough.

Maybe somebody else will come and take my place at your house or in the Young Trib Force. I hope they do. If you care for them half as much as you cared for me, they'll be really happy.

Ryan's strength was running out. The light in the room was fading.

Promise me you'll take care of Phoenix. Tell Chaya and Shelly and Mark and John that I was thinking of them. I hope you all made it through the earthquake. I'll never forget you.

Love,
Ryan

Ryan put the pen down and wept. The nurse returned and removed the pad. She took his temperature and gave him more medicine.

"When do you think somebody could take this letter?" Ryan asked.

"I'm not sure," the nurse said. "But we'll get it to someone you know."

"Promise?" Ryan said.

The nurse looked at him and smiled. "I'll take it myself if I have to," she said.

The nurse turned to leave.

"Wait," Ryan said. "I wanted to ask you something."

"You need a drink, something to eat?" the nurse said.

"No," Ryan said. "It's about God."

"I don't think we have a chaplain here," the nurse said.

"It's not that," Ryan said. "I want to know if you believe in him. Do you know God?"

Chaya tasted blood again. She had read stories of people on the brink of death and what it was like, but she hadn't pictured it this way. She wanted her father to believe in Christ, pray, and be rescued. But after her description of Jesus as Messiah, Mr. Stein didn't speak. He either went to sleep or ignored her.

The sunlight faded. Soon it would get colder, and she knew she could not survive. Chaya wheezed and coughed.

God, please help my father come to the truth before it is too late, she prayed.

In her brief time as a Christian, Chaya had memorized many sections of Scripture. Bruce Barnes suggested she commit key portions of the book of Revelation to memory. As she lay in the dust of her prison, she recalled the apostle John's words. He described a silence in heaven, followed by an angel who stood at the golden altar before the throne of God.

"The smoke of the incense, mixed with the prayers of the saints, ascended up to God from the altar where the angel had poured them out. Then the angel filled the incense burner with fire from the altar and threw it down upon the earth; and thunder crashed, lightning flashed, and there was a terrible earthquake.

"Then the seven angels with the seven trumpets prepared to blow their mighty blasts."

The words brought a strange comfort. She felt the earthquake was her final earthly glimpse of fulfilled Scripture. She knew the judgments of God would get progressively worse, and she was relieved she wouldn't have to experience what was coming next.

Still, to die without seeing her father accept Christ overwhelmed Chaya. She began to weep for him.

"Why are you crying?" Mr. Stein said after a few moments.

"I weep for you, Father," Chaya said. "I have prayed for you since the day I made my decision."

"And I have prayed that you would come back," Mr. Stein said.

"Your heart is so hard," Chaya said. "You

are like the pharaoh in Egypt. Though you have sign after sign, you still will not believe."

"You compare me to an Egyptian pharaoh," Mr. Stein said, "and I say you have forsaken the God of Israel and gone after other gods."

Chaya wanted to argue more, but she knew it would do no good. Her father had made his decision.

"If you make it through this," Chaya said, "would you please find my friends and tell them what happened?"

"You are going to be fine," Mr. Stein said. "Just rest. Don't try to talk."

"Promise me," Chaya said weakly.

"I will find them," Mr. Stein said.

"Thank you," Chaya said.

She closed her eyes. The pain made her shiver. She thought of her mother and clutched the broach tightly.

"Father?" Chaya whispered.

"Shh," Mr. Stein said. "Don't talk. I think I hear someone outside."

"I love you," Chaya said.

TEN

Decision Time

9:22 P.M.

VICKI was exhausted when the girls made it to the shelter. The camp was a series of tents salvaged from a nearby sporting goods store. Volunteers handed out sleeping bags and blankets to those straggling in. Families huddled over small fires.

While Shelly and Darrion scoped out a place to sleep, Vicki went to the large tent in the center. The injured lay on air mattresses or on the ground. As she entered, a young woman let out a piercing scream.

"No!" she yelled as she gripped the hand of a pale woman.

Vicki found a nurse and asked about Ryan. The nurse showed her a list of the dead.

"That's the best I can do for you," the woman said.

Vicki thanked her and scanned the names. There was no Ryan Daley. She walked through the tent but couldn't find him.

She rejoined Darrion and Shelly in a small, two-person tent. They held steaming cups of soup and bread. Shelly had a bandage for her ear.

"No spoons," Darrion said, "but it's pretty good."

They handed Vicki a cup, and she dipped the bread in the broth. The meal was simple but satisfying.

"You think we can all fit in here?" Vicki said.

"We'll have to," Shelly said. "It's supposed to get chilly, and they could only spare two blankets."

"The soup was good," Darrion said when she had finished, "but I'd go for some shrimp cocktail right now."

Shelly cackled. "You've spent too much time at the country club," she said. "I'd go for a cheeseburger. Extra cheese."

"Stop," Vicki said. "I was happy with the soup. Now you guys are making me hungry for dessert."

"Cheesecake," Darrion said.

"Apple pie and ice cream," Shelly said. "My mom, when she was sober, used to bake it from scratch. Then the ice cream would melt on top."

"Did your mother ever . . . I mean, was she . . . ," Darrion stammered.

"Was she a Christian?" Shelly said.

"If you don't want to talk about it, I understand," Darrion said.

"It's OK," Shelly said. "Vicki knows I tried to talk to her. Sometimes she'd listen, but most of the time she'd get mad."

Vicki shook her head and shivered.

"What is it?" Darrion said.

"The graveyard," Vicki said. "I can't stop thinking about it."

"I'd still be screaming if it had happened to me," Darrion said.

"Plus, Mrs. Jenness," Vicki said. "It helps to talk."

"Then go ahead," Shelly said.

"When we were on the bridge, it was like she was a little kid," Vicki said. "She froze. Couldn't move. Then we were in the water and I got out. But I felt guilty leaving her."

"You can't force people to do what they need to do," Shelly said.

"The look on her face will haunt me forever," Vicki said.

"You know what I think?" Darrion said. "I think we ought to be thankful for the miracle that you're alive. You could have gone down with her."

"I was so scared," Vicki said. "I could tell God was helping me because I just seemed to go on autopilot. I didn't even think about what could happen; I just did it."

Shelly and Darrion recounted their experiences. Finally Shelly said, "I wonder how everybody else is. We know Mark's OK, but what about Lionel and Ryan?"

"And Judd," Darrion said.

Judd.

The mention of his name made Vicki tremble. "If I know Judd," Vicki said, "he's out there somewhere in a lot of trouble, but he's alive."

The girls stopped talking and listened to the crackling fires and the moans and cries that came from the main tent. Vicki thought of Judd. She imagined what it would be like to tell him how she really felt about him. She felt he was alive. Whether he was in the custody of the Global Community or not, he had to be alive. She wished he were here. He would know how to find Ryan.

"I think we ought to pray," Vicki said.

And they did until all three fell asleep.

Judd nearly lost his breath when he saw the men staring at him. His first instinct was to run. He was in danger.

"Are you GC?" one man said.

"No," Judd said.

"What are you doing up here then?" another man said.

"I'm trying to get home," Judd said. "I thought I could cross over the dam up ahead."

The first man motioned to the others to move away. They walked toward Judd and down the side of the hill.

"Middle of the dam fell in," the man said. "Can't get across that unless you jump it."

"I can try," Judd said. "Looks like my only choice."

"Probably is for now," the man said. "But we could use a machine like this. It'd help us and our families."

"Families?" Judd said.

"When the quake hit, a few of us ran up here for safety. Caves all over this area. A couple of them collapsed. Those who survived are in that one, but we don't have many supplies."

Judd untied the bag on the back of the bike and handed it to the man. "It's not much," Judd said, "but it's all I have. I need the bike. You keep the food."

"It's dark now," the man said. "Why don't you stay with us for the night? We have a fire. You'll be warm."

"That's kind of you," Judd said, "but I have to keep going."

"How?" the man said. "You'll kill yourself if you can't see anything."

"I want to take a look at what I'm up against," Judd said.

Judd started the motorcycle and looked back at the man. Members of his family peered out of the darkness of the cave. Judd gunned the engine and headed for the top of the ridge.

He knew the man was right. He had to stop at some point and rest, but he didn't want to stay here. Something about the people unnerved him.

The dam was ten feet wide and nearly a hundred yards across. The moon shone a ghostly glow on the water below. Judd stopped the bike and walked to the center of the dam. A gap of about fifteen feet had opened.

I could put a tree across here and crawl over, Judd thought. *But I'd never cross on the bike.*

The man was right about jumping the gap. Judd had done that type of thing as a kid on a regular bicycle, but he'd had a ramp. He would have to jump this without one.

The rest of the bridge seemed to be in good shape. There were cracks and a few pieces of loose concrete, but there didn't seem to be a danger of collapse. Judd noticed the earthquake had pushed the other side of the dam slightly lower and forward. That would help, but it also meant he would have to jump at an angle.

Judd retreated and looked at his target from a distance. *If I miss, I'm dead*, he thought. *I could camp here and jump in the morning, but those guys might decide they want more than just my food.*

Judd decided to take the risk. He started the motorcycle and rode to the edge. He could clear the gap at forty miles an hour. But he wouldn't know if he could make that speed until he tried.

He drove up the bank and revved the engine. "Do or die," Judd said.

Lionel asked to see the GC leader. The man returned a few minutes later and sat by Lionel's bed. He was carrying a leather case.

"What's up?" the man said.

"I've thought about it enough," Lionel said. "I don't need to wait until tomorrow. I'm in. I want to be a part of what you're doing, and I'll go wherever you send me."

"That's good news," the man said. He pulled some papers out of the case. "I have you paired with Conrad Graham."

"He's a friend," Lionel said.

"Good. We're sending you both to Chicago. Maybe you'll piece things together personally once you're back near your home."

The man had Lionel sign some documents. Then he unzipped a smaller pouch and took out a tiny phone.

"You'll keep in touch with this," the man said. "Solar powered. Once the lines are in place, you'll be able to talk with anybody you need to in the world."

"When do I leave?" Lionel said.

"You'll need to go through a bit more training," the man said. He pulled something else out of the case. "And you'll need to get familiar with this."

The man pulled out a gun. Lionel knew accepting it meant he would be part of the Global Community. He hesitated a moment.

"It won't bite you," the man said.

Lionel took the gun. He felt its weight. He knew his life had changed forever.

Ryan was glad the nurse had listened to his story, but he was frustrated. His thoughts were jumbled, and he couldn't remember some of the verses he had memorized.

The nurse felt his head and wiped it with a

towel. She took his temperature and strapped something around his arm.

"Your blood pressure's falling," the nurse said. "I'll need to get the doctor."

Ryan rolled his head back and forth on the pillow. *What is that verse?* he thought. *Something about God and the world.*

When the nurse returned with the doctor, Ryan was excited.

"I remember now," Ryan said. "Not word for word, but—"

"Just lie still," the doctor said.

"He's been going on like this," the nurse said.

"God loved the world," Ryan said, "and he loved it so much he gave his Son."

"His pulse is erratic," the doctor said.

"That's Jesus," Ryan said. "And anybody who believes in him won't die. They'll have eternal life."

"Should I get someone?" the nurse said.

"There's no one who can help him now," the doctor said.

"You have to trust him," Ryan said. "Do you believe in Jesus?"

The room spun. Ryan closed his eyes. He wished Judd were here. Or Vicki. He thought of Phoenix and the long bike rides they used to take. The dog was beside him all the way.

Ryan opened his eyes. "Am I going to die?" he said.

"We're doing everything we can," the doctor said.

"Doesn't answer my question," Ryan said. The doctor was changing the medication in Ryan's IV. Ryan grabbed the man's coat and held on.

"I asked if you think I'm gonna die," Ryan said.

The doctor looked at him gravely. "I choose to believe all my patients will make it," the doctor said, "but I'll admit I have my doubts."

Ryan let go. "It's not so bad," he said. "I have some friends waiting for me up there."

"Lie still and try not to talk," the doctor said.

Ryan closed his eyes again. He was so hot. So tired. He just wanted to sleep. He wanted to go home.

Mr. Stein screamed for help. Finally someone came. Flashlight beams lit the room. Layer after layer of debris had to be cleared. Finally the rescuers reached Mr. Stein. He was cold, and he knew he had lost a lot of blood.

"Don't worry about me; find my daughter," Mr. Stein said. He pointed.

It had been some time since Chaya had spoken. She had passed out, then revived, only to pester him again to consider Jesus. It seemed the only thing on her mind.

The men lifted the beam on top of Mr. Stein enough to pull him from the rubble. He grabbed one of the flashlights.

"Uh, sir, you might not want to look over there," one of the men said.

"I have to find my daughter," Mr. Stein said.

The light flashed on something. Mr. Stein gasped. The broach. A few inches away he saw his daughter's delicate hand.

"Help me here!" Mr. Stein yelled, but he was in no shape to move, let alone pull his daughter from the rubble.

Mr. Stein picked up the broach as the men tried to remove Chaya. A wall shifted, and plaster fell on them.

"It's not safe in here," a man said. "We have to get out."

"Not without her," Mr. Stein said.

"You can stay if you want," the man said.

Mr. Stein knelt and cradled Chaya's head in his lap. He felt for a pulse, but there was none. He brushed the hair from her face and cleaned a streak of blood from her mouth.

"You look just like your mother," Mr. Stein said as he wept. "So beautiful."

He looked at the night sky through the shambles of his home. Stars and the bright moon.

"Why?" he said softly. "Why did you take the only one left to me?"

Louder and louder he wailed. "Why? Why?"

Epilogue

JUDD raced down the bank to the dam. He was up to thirty miles an hour when his front tire hit a stick. Judd swerved and slammed on the brakes. He stopped a few feet short of the edge. *Maybe this was God's way of telling me to stop*, he thought.

Judd turned around and cleared the path, making sure there were no hidden obstacles. He took the bike farther back and revved the engine again.

"If you don't want me to do this, God," Judd said out loud, "then stop me."

Judd plunged down the hill and picked up speed. He was going thirty-five before he made it to the pavement. He knew he had enough speed, but something felt wrong.

He was still bouncing when he hit the concrete, like he was on uneven ground. The speedometer said 40 mph. Judd slammed on the brakes. He heard thunder and felt the dam rocking.

Aftershock, Judd thought.

He was nearing the edge, sliding, burning rubber, when he realized he was not going to stop. He put the bike down and slid with it to the edge. The motorcycle, still running, plunged over the side. Judd put out his hands and grabbed the railing. His momentum nearly took him over, but he managed to hold on, his feet dangling over the edge.

He looked below and saw the green motorcycle splash into the murky water. It floated a moment, then sank.

Judd held on. The water seemed to rush by faster. He couldn't survive the fall, and the current would take him if he did. He tried to get a foothold on the side of the dam, but the concrete crumbled with each try.

OK, Judd thought, *I guess I wasn't supposed to do that. Now what?*

He was alone, hanging on for his life, the earth shaking again, and there was no one to help him.

ABOUT THE AUTHORS

Jerry B. Jenkins (www.jerryjenkins.com) is the writer of the Left Behind series. He is author of more than one hundred books, of which eleven have reached the *New York Times* best-seller list. Former vice president for publishing for the Moody Bible Institute of Chicago, he also served many years as editor of *Moody* magazine and is now Moody's writer-at-large.

His writing has appeared in publications as varied as *Reader's Digest, Parade,* in-flight magazines, and many Christian periodicals. He has written books in four genres: biography, marriage and family, fiction for children, and fiction for adults.

Jenkins's biographies include books with Hank Aaron, Bill Gaither, Luis Palau, Walter Payton, Orel Hershiser, Nolan Ryan, Brett Butler, and Billy Graham, among many others.

Eight of his apocalyptic novels—*Left Behind, Tribulation Force, Nicolae, Soul Harvest, Apollyon, Assassins, The Indwelling,* and *The Mark*—have appeared on the Christian Booksellers Association's best-selling fiction list and the *Publishers Weekly* religion best-seller list. *Left Behind* was nominated for Book of the Year by the Evangelical Christian Publishers Association in 1997, 1998, 1999, and 2000. *The Indwelling* was number one on the *New York Times* best-seller list for four consecutive weeks.

As a marriage and family author and speaker, Jenkins has been a frequent guest on Dr. James Dobson's *Focus on the Family* radio program.

Jerry is also the writer of the nationally syndicated sports story comic strip *Gil Thorp,* distributed to newspapers across the United States by Tribune Media Services.

Jerry and his wife, Dianna, live in Colorado.

Dr. Tim LaHaye (www.timlahaye.com), who conceived the idea of fictionalizing an account of the Rapture and the Tribulation, is a noted author, minister, and nationally recognized speaker on Bible prophecy. He is the founder of both Tim LaHaye Ministries and The Pre-Trib Research Center. Presently Dr. LaHaye speaks at many of the major Bible prophecy conferences in the U.S. and Canada, where his nine current prophecy books are very popular.

Dr. LaHaye holds a doctor of ministry degree from Western Theological Seminary and the doctor of literature degree from Liberty University. For twenty-five years he pastored one of the nation's outstanding churches in San Diego, which grew to three locations. It was during that time that he founded two accredited Christian high schools, a Christian school system of ten schools, and Christian Heritage College.

Dr. LaHaye has written over forty books, with over 30 million copies in print in thirty-three languages. He has written books on a wide variety of subjects, such as family life, temperaments, and Bible prophecy. His current fiction works, written with Jerry Jenkins—*Left Behind, Tribulation Force, Nicolae, Soul Harvest, Apollyon, Assassins, The Indwelling,* and *The Mark*—have all reached number one on the Christian best-seller charts. Other works by Dr. LaHaye are *Spirit-Controlled Temperament; How to Be Happy Though Married; Revelation Unveiled; Understanding the Last Days; Rapture under Attack; Are We Living in the End Times?;* and the youth fiction series Left Behind: The Kids.

He is the father of four grown children and grandfather of nine. Snow skiing, waterskiing, motorcycling, golfing, vacationing with family, and jogging are among his leisure activities.

The Future Is Clear

Check out the exciting Left Behind: The Kids series

#1: The Vanishings

#2: Second Chance

#3: Through the Flames

#4: Facing the Future

#5: Nicolae High

#6: The Underground

#7: Busted!

#8: Death Strike

#9: The Search

#10: On the Run

#11: Into the Storm

#12: Earthquake!

#13: The Showdown

#14: Judgment Day

#15: Battling the Commander

#16: Fire from Heaven

#17: Terror in the Stadium

#18: Darkening Skies

Books #19 and #20 coming soon!

Discover the latest about the Left Behind series and complete line of products at

www.leftbehind.com